I0687012

Untold

SISTERHOOD CHRONICLES 3

ANITA DAVIS

This is a work of fiction. Names, characters, businesses, places, events and incidents are either the products of the author's imagination or used in a fictitious manner. Any resemblance to actual persons, living or dead, or actual events is purely coincidental.

Copyright © 2016 Anita Davis

All Rights Reserved. No part of this publication may be reproduced, stored in a retrieval system, or transmitted, in any form or in any means – by electronic, mechanical, photocopying, recording or otherwise – without prior written permission.

ISBN-10: 1-946721-05-0
ISBN-13: 978-1-946721-05-1

Books may be purchased in quantity by contacting the author Anita Davis:
Set Apart Publishing
PO Box 39229
Chicago, IL 60659
or by email at authoranitadavis@gmail.com

ACKNOWLEDGEMENTS

I dedicate this book to Gabby who was distraught with not getting the ending she wanted in "It's Complicated". LOL.

A special thank you to Teoahnna Mayo for helping me better understand social workers and what they do. Thank you for answering all of my questions.

Also thank you to my way back when buddy, Officer Darrise Richardson, aka Main, for helping me with the specifics of the law.

Thank you, Alicia "The Pretty Brown Eyed Reader" for your feedback and kindness towards me.

Thank you to Michelle Chester of EBM Professional Services. I am so grateful to have you as my editor. You have no idea how you going back and forth with me while editing or just responding to my random texts and emails blesses me. You simply are great.

Thank you to my readers who anticipate book after book from me. Especially Shawntell Langford who reached out to me looking for the release date of this book. Your enjoyment of my books melts my heart.

Thank you all so much.

ENJOY

In all secrets there is a kind of guilt, however beautiful or joyful they may be, or for what good end they may be set to serve. Secrecy means evasion, and evasion means a problem to the moral mind.
~Gilbert Parker

1

Renee sat at her desk staring at the dark chocolate face of the latest child to break her heart.

It had been a while since a case as bad as the one before her had come across her desk. She breathed a deep sigh of frustration as she thumbed through the pages of the report. Being a social worker, she had seen some horrific things happen to kids in the homes of their birth parents as well as homes they were temporarily placed in. She'd even seen an unhealthy share of finalized adoptions end bad for the kids.

Her current case pierced her core as it brewed so many what if questions to memories from her past, but she pulled herself from her yesteryears to focus on the case before her. Perusing the notes in the file, she zoomed in on her anecdotal of the first time she had to visit the boy's home after her office received an

1

anonymous call of neglect and abuse at his residence. She remembered pulling up to the house and if the outside of it was any indication of what was going on inside, she surmised that she would have to remove Brandon from the home immediately. The address given by the anonymous caller was located in a neighborhood Chicagoans refer to as K-Town, seeing as though the streets running north to south in the neighborhood's circumference all start with a K.

Any other social worker might have been leery of going to the address because it was one of Chicago's high crime neighborhoods. However, her zeal as an advocate for disenfranchised youth and her belief in God that He covered her every move put her at ease following the lead.

She sat in her sedan with her head going back and forth between the address on the file on her lap versus the tattered address on the building. The numbers matched and she knew she was on the right street. The six-unit building looked like it was abandoned. As if a bulldozer would be coming down the street any minute, park in either of the abandoned and littered lots adjacent to the building, and demolish it to its foundation. Studying the building, she saw that five of the units had broken windows. The sight of it made her believe that no one could inhabit the units and keep warm in the winter with such big gaping holes allowing cold, harsh Chicago winds to blow through them as desired. There definitely could be no reprieve or even comfort from the balmy summer they were having if anyone did inhabit one of the units. Colorful graffiti was sporadically splattered over the building with what seemed like at least three gangs trying to label the edifice as their own.

Her attention was pulled from the building when a man tapped on her driver's side window. She couldn't see his face and she refused to let her window down. After another tap on her window, he finally knelt down to be eye level with her. "Shorty, whatchu need?" He held his pants up with one hand and a cigarette up to his mouth with the other. He stared at her intently.

Although she knew she had God on her side, she also knew He gave her wisdom with what to do in certain situations. She refused to let her window down and instead cleared her throat and spoke up loud enough to be heard. "I'm with DCFS. There's supposed to be a child in that building I have to check up on."

He stepped back from the car so he would no longer have to kneel to see her face. He flicked his lit cigarette off into the street. "'Bout time y'all came to check up on lil' man." He stuffed his hands into his pocket and relaxed his shoulders.

Sensing that the man was no longer a threat to her, Renee stepped out of her car with her folder close to her chest and pressed the lock button on her key fob. She smiled, looking at the man who was still standing in the street. "So you know the boy?"

He nodded his head slightly. "Yeah, I know lil' B. I walk him to school sometimes whenever his trifling momma gets him dressed for it."

With raised eyebrows, Renee looked over her shoulder at the building before turning to speak to the man again. "So someone actually lives in that building?"

He chuckled, staring Renee up and down. "Yeah, ma. Everybody ain't got it good."

"I know." Her voice was barely audible.

"Don't worry. You ain't gotta be afraid of us around here, especially not me. I got you. I'll watch your car for you while you go in there and check up on the lil' homie."

"Thanks." Renee gave him a half smile and shifted on her feet to make her way towards the building.

"Aye?"

She looked back at the man beckoning for her attention.

"I hope y'all come out with him this time. Stop letting his momma get him back." He looked over his shoulder to see if he had a customer waiting on him. He walked back over to the corner he was perched on before Renee's arrival.

"I hope so, too," she mumbled with her back towards him again as she made her way to the building. She carefully walked past the rusted, black iron fence that probably once secured the property, but with it missing many of its spindles, she knew it no longer served its purpose.

She made her way to the one step that elevated the first floor from ground level, and although there were buttons serving as doorbells on a panel at eye level to the right of her, the unstable door in front of her was wide open. *Should I ring the doorbell to 1A anyway?* She rang it in hopes of alerting someone in the apartment that they had a visitor. After five minutes of waiting with no response, she decided to make her way through the urine-scented hallway and up the rickety stairs to apartment 1A. The further she went the more deplorable the smell was. She made it to 1A and took short breaths trying not to inhale too much of the scent that had intensified with a hint of feces and mold.

She knocked on the door.

No one answered.

She knocked again.

The notes in the file reported that the worker previously assigned to the case had been to the apartment daily for the past two weeks with no one answering the door. She knew she needed to speak with the mother that day. She wouldn't rest easy that night unless she was able to confirm the boy's well-being.

She knocked on the door again and with the third knock it slowly opened. "Hello." She spoke into the sliver of the door that was open. She held her breath for a second looking at the piles of filth strewn over what should have been a clean inhabitable living room, but instead, it seemed to be the building's massive garbage can. "Hello." She called out again and leaned on the door, but a weight pressing the door in opposition of her let her know it wouldn't be so easy to get in. "Hello. My name is Renee and I'm with the Department of Children and Family Services."

With her admission, a little waving hand peeked from behind the door.

"Brandon, is that you? Will you let me in?"

"Okay," a soft, croaky voice whispered and stepped from behind the door, giving Renee clearance to open the door all of the way.

Renee stepped into the apartment and had to take a moment to gather her wits. The stench in the hallway paled in comparison to the smell permeating through the apartment. If she could articulate the odor accosting her, she would've described it as piles of feces festering in a desert. The late spring heat wave that had made Chicago its residence seemed to cook the horrific smells to a boiling point of disgust for anyone that entered the space.

She shook off her discomfort of being there and shifted her focus to Brandon. Stooping to be at eye level with him, she spoke up, "Brandon, are you okay?"

He shrugged his shoulders with his head low.

"Are you home alone?"

He shook his head from side to side.

"Well, where is your mother then?"

He lifted his head and arm simultaneously and pointed to the back of the apartment.

Renee stood to her feet assessing where Brandon had pointed. Three doors lined the hallway on the left of it and one was affixed to the right of it. She looked back down at him. "Okay, Brandon. You stay here. I'll go see where your mother is."

Since no one had come to the front door yet questioning why she was there, she didn't know what she would find when she went in the direction in which Brandon pointed. If he hadn't already, she didn't want him to discover what she might when she made her way back there.

7

She stepped over trash and soiled clothes as she made her way down the hall peeking in each open door. The first and second doors on the left side of the hallway proved to be empty bedrooms just as littered as the first room she entered in the apartment. The only door on the right of the hallway was an outdated and filthy bathroom. As she neared the last door on the left of the hallway, she paused to suck in as much air as she could hold in her stomach. The smell coming from it proved to be the worst she had encountered up to that point.

"Yvette? Ms. Smith, are you in there?" She peeked into the room to find who she assumed to be Yvette face up on the stained mattress. Foam had dried up on her mouth. Renee shook her head as she stared at what seemed to be the cause of the woman's demise. There was a rubber strap tied around one arm, a used needle in her other hand, and a small folding table to the right of her. Renee knew enough to know what Yvette last did causing her recent state— heroine.

She was no medical expert, but given the fact that she had to have been in the room for several minutes and not once had Yvette's chest heave up and down, she gathered that Yvette was dead.

She backed out of the room and called 911. She walked back up to where Brandon still stood and stooped to be eye level with him again. "Brandon, remember my name is Renee?"

He slowly nodded.

"You're going to be coming with me, okay?"

Renee knew she needed to get Brandon out of the house as she heard the sirens in the distance. She didn't want him to witness them taking his mother out on a stretcher with a white sheet covering her face. She grabbed his four year old hand to walk him down the stairs, but when she looked down to see that he didn't have shoes on, she knew she couldn't allow him to walk on the broken glass scattered in the hallway. She scanned the room but didn't spot a single clean thing she could put on him to take him out of the house, so she scooped him up into her arms with nothing but a stained T-shirt on and soiled underpants and carried him down the stairs.

The sirens were growing louder and she could see the red and white lights reflecting off of buildings down the street. She picked up her speed to get Brandon to her car. By the time she made it out to the gate, the guy she had spoken with earlier rushed from the corner and over to her. He looked down the street to see the ambulance nearing him and then looked back at her. It was no surprise that they would get to the house so soon since there was a hospital not too far from the apartment building. "You need help with him?" he asked.

Luckily she always kept a car seat and a booster seat in her car. "I need help getting the booster seat out of my trunk." She held Brandon closer to her as she popped her lock.

The guy rushed ahead of her and pulled the booster seat from the trunk and put it in the back seat. She placed Brandon in the seat and secured him there. Through it all Brandon remained silent. He didn't shed one tear.

"You want me to stay with him while you go talk to them?" He pointed to the EMT's exiting their vehicle and making their way up to the building.

"Will you?"

He nodded his approval.

"Thanks." One would think that Renee would've opposed leaving Brandon with the stranger but she sensed in her spirit that he would do Brandon no harm and not to mention her car was barely fifty feet away from where the EMT's stood. She walked over to them before they made it the hallway door. "Hi, I'm the one that called it in."

"Okay," the EMT nearest her responded.

"I'm with DCFS. I have her son and I want to get him out of here before you all bring her out, but I'll make sure that I include everything that I noticed in the home today in my report. And if there's anything else you need from me, please call this number." She handed the EMT her business card before she walked off.

Renee brought herself back into the present with the knowledge that that was four years ago and things had only gotten worse for Brandon.

She got up from her desk to stretch and to use the restroom. She opened the door to her office and stepped out to see many of her coworkers busy on their phones dealing with cases of their own and a few of them even had clients they were assisting at their cubicles. She smiled and nodded at those who caught her eye as she made her way to the bathroom.

She was headed back to her office in no time. Closing the door behind her, she thanked God that she actually had an office rather than just a cubicle. Having four walls and a door to her personal space at work provided her with the privacy she needed to pray in the manner she was accustomed to. Renee, as well as many of her coworkers, knew that it was her calling to do what she was doing, helping kids in need.

She never took any of her cases lightly. The moment her division got a new one, even before she opened the file, she said a prayer that God would go before her and shift things so that her office could bring a favorable outcome to the child that was listed in the file.

She was blessed to get a job in her field the moment she graduated from college and returned home to Chicago. With her skills being sharp and her passion being evident from her very first case, she quickly moved up the ranks in the investigative department. Although she had the label of being the supervisor of her department, she also enjoyed doing field work and not just delegating assignments to those in her stead. Everyone in her department admired and respected her for such.

She sat back in her seat again and shook her head in frustration. She just couldn't understand how she still hadn't found the best situation for Brandon.

After she had taken him from his mom that day, she took him back to the office and cleaned him up. She knew from his file and previous attempts to locate family members that there was no next of kin that could take the boy in, but that didn't stifle her because the department had a list of what she thought were reliable foster homes. Back then, she dialed the first number on the list and within hours she had placed the boy into the temporary custody of a middle aged woman who already had two other foster children in her home.

Renee thought that Brandon would be okay there until she was able to secure a family, or at least an individual willing to adopt him, but by the end of the week the foster mother called her back to come and get Brandon.

Renee huffed as she rested her elbows on her desk staring at her notes from the day she had to go rescue Brandon for the second time. She remembered pulling up to the two flat located not too far from the green line elevated train merely streets away from Austin Ave in the Austin area of Chicago, the west side of town. The house was situated on a quiet street and it was far more appealing than the building she initially rescued him from. The foster mother didn't say much over the phone other than she couldn't do much to help what was happening to the boy and to please come get him. Renee got out of her car and made her way to the front porch. She rang the doorbell, and said a silent prayer that God would fix whatever was transpiring on the other side of the door.

If Brandon could no longer be there, she needed God to open up a safe haven for him immediately. He already experienced so much tragedy in his life at such a young age, she didn't know how much more his fragile yet developing psyche could take before the circumstances of his life turned him into someone he was never destined to be.

She remembered standing at the door and hearing footsteps nearing it knowing that she didn't have time to allot to her personal worries, again. Brandon required her undivided attention.

"Hello." The woman with freckles sprinkling the bridge of her nose opened the door and welcomed Renee into her first floor apartment.

Renee stepped in noting that nothing seemed visibly wrong or threatening for Brandon there.

"Please come in and have a seat." The woman motioned for Renee to sit on a loveseat in the living room.

Renee obliged.

"Would you like something to drink?" She smiled at Renee as she stood in the entryway between the living room and the dining room.

"No, thank you."

"Okay, well..." She sat and placed her hands in her lap as she prepared herself to speak to Renee.

"Brandon is a great little boy, in spite of the neglect he's experienced at his age."

Renee saw sadness in the woman's eyes.

"I love having him here."

Renee scooted closer to the edge of her seat. "Well then, what's the problem?"

The woman breathed a deep, loud sigh. "The problem is with one of the other foster kids I have here, Eric being the main one."

Renee knew of the fourteen year old the woman was speaking of. "What's the problem with Eric?"

"Well you already know I've had Eric here for a year. I got Rashad three months after Eric. Eric didn't too much like when Rashad came here at first. He wanted to be the only kid with me, but he ended up taking a liking to Rashad since he's close to him in age. They get along just fine now."

Renee's face scrunched in confusion. She had heard it all when it came to what happened in foster homes, but she wanted to give this particular situation the benefit of the doubt before she jumped to any conclusions.

The woman could see that Renee was confused so she continued on. "Well, Eric wants me to adopt him. He's just used to it being the three of us. He has a routine around here and I'm able to give him and Rashad all of my free time, but since Brandon has been here, he's required a lot of my attention. I'm trying to get him used to going to school and whatnot."

Renee smiled at the compassion she heard for the boys in the woman's voice before she noticed the woman's eyes misting.

15

"It seems as if Eric is being abusive to Brandon."

Renee's heart jumped for Brandon as she shifted uncomfortably on the edge of the twill couch. "How do you know that?"

"Brandon was talkative and trying to interact with the boys on day one, but by day four he had become even more withdrawn than he was when you first brought him here." She tried to steady her shaking knees with her hands. "I've been dealing with foster kids for a while, I know the signs. I give Brandon his baths at night. He didn't have any markings on him the first night he was here, but that fourth night I bathed him, he had bruises all over his back." She tried to rid her face of the tears streaming it.

Renee knew the woman had an impeccable record as a foster mother. She didn't want to question the woman's character, but it was a part of her job. "Ms. Turner, are you sure that having three foster kids here with you is not overwhelming? Maybe one day, out of frustration you called yourself trying to discipline Brandon and it got out of hand?"

Ms. Turner jumped out her seat. "Ms. Williams! You all have been assigning kids to me long enough to know that I would never lay a hand on them no matter how they behaved. We've talked plenty of times before and as passionate as you are about helping these kids, so am I."

Renee stood and slowly walked to the woman. She looked her in her eyes. "Ms. Turner, you're right. I apologize for my accusation, but you know getting to the bottom of the issue is my ultimate responsibility." Her eyes pleaded with the woman's for understanding.

"I know. I know." Ms. Turner hugged herself tighter.

"Let's have a seat again," Renee suggested.

Both of the ladies took their seats and Ms. Turner continued on. "To get right to the point, I believe, no, let me rephrase that, I know that Eric is hurting Brandon because he doesn't want him here."

"Are you sure it's Eric's doing it?"

"Yes. When I saw the bruises that night on Brandon, I questioned him but he wouldn't tell me who hurt him. I went up to the school with him the next day and talked to the teachers about it. His teacher informed me that because of Brandon's age, there is always an adult around the kids in the classroom and she and her assistant hadn't seen any of the other kids in the classroom harm him. I left him and went to work.

"I had it setup with the boys that they pick Brandon up after they get out, since they are all in the same school building, and bring him home with them. I get from work maybe five minutes after they make it. Well, by the time I made it home that day, Brandon was balled up in a corner crying. When I called him over to me, his shirt was bloody and torn and his nose was bleeding."

Renee shook her head in sadness.

"I called Eric and Rashad into the living room and asked Brandon in front of them what happened, but he wouldn't speak up. I asked Eric next but he wouldn't say anything. By the time I turned to Rashad, he began confessing that he tried to stop Eric but Eric threatened to get him next if he didn't butt out."

"Ms. Turner, why didn't you call us when you first suspected it?"

She nervously twisted the ring on her pointer finger. "I know I should have, but I was just thinking that if I could figure out what was going on, I could resolve it and be able to keep all three boys here."

"I appreciate that, Ms. Turner, but you know it's your duty to contact us the moment you suspect something nefarious with the kids we entrust to your care."

"I know, I'm sorry. I didn't but that's why I called last night after Rashad confessed so that you could come here first thing this morning. I took off from work and all." She clutched her arms to her chest.

"So, you know this means I may have to remove all three of the boys from the home until we figure out what's best for each. Legal action may have to be taken against Eric."

Again Ms. Turner jumped from her seat and paced the floor. "Ms. Williams, please don't do that."

"Ms. Turner, you know any time a complaint is made, a thorough investigation has to be made before we decide what's best for the children."

Ms. Turner rushed over to Renee and sat on the coffee table in front of her. She reached out and clasped Renee's hands into hers. "Ms. Williams, I know it was wrong what Eric did, but you have to remember what he's been through, too, in his fourteen years on this earth. His life started out much like Brandon's. Abuse is all he knows. It was rough for him when he first came to be with me. He acted out in school, but when he realized that I really did care for him and wouldn't abandon him like everyone else had, he turned around real quick. He's even been a good example to Rashad," she lowered her voice, "aside from this past week. I know you need to do your investigation, but please, please, can I have Eric and Rashad back?

"If they don't stay with me, they may very well end up in the streets on the path that will either lead to jail or even worse, the cemetery. I've even started the paperwork to adopt them, you know that. I would love to have Brandon here, too, but if I had to choose and if you see fit to let me get them again, I'd rather just keep Eric and Rashad. I'm certain you can find another home for Brandon. People generally like the younger kids anyway." She gripped Renee's hands harder. Seeing the stoic look on Renee's face prompted her to keep talking. "I just know that I will have a big impact on the way Eric and Rashad turn out. I wouldn't know what to do with myself if I turned on the news one day to see that either one of them were killed or hauled off to jail after they were snatched out of my care."

Renee empathized with Ms. Turner and as odd as her logic may have sounded to others, in the world of social workers, foster parents, and kids, it made sense to her. She stood up with Ms. Turner's hands still locked on hers, forcing her to stand as well. "I hear what you're saying, more importantly, I hear your heart. Eric and Rashad can stay here while I complete the investigation, but I'll have to remove Brandon in the meantime."

"And can you see if Eric won't be punished for what he did?" Ms. Turner's eyes widened with hope.

"I'll have to talk that over with his social worker and my boss."

"Oh please, will you?"

"I'll try."

Renee came back to the present clicking her tongue to the roof of her mouth trying to provide moisture to it. She was thirsty. She reached into the mini-fridge next to her desk and grabbed a bottled water. She didn't need to look at the file again to know what had happened to Brandon after she left with him from Ms. Turner's house. Eric and Rashad were able to stay in the home, and were ultimately adopted by Ms. Turner, but she couldn't return Brandon back to Ms. Turner's care. He had been placed with the Millers, the next reason his file was on her desk once again, four years later.

There was a knock on Renee's office door preventing her from continuing down memory lane with the specifics of Brandon's file. "Come in," she called out to whoever was on the other side.

The door swung open and one of Renee's subordinates, Amina, peeked her head in. "Hey, Renee."

"Hey." Renee swiveled in her chair to completely face Amina.

"I was just wondering if you wanted to head to lunch with a few of us."

21

"Thanks, but I brought my lunch."

Being comfortable with invading Renee's personal space, Amina stepped into the office. "Renee, you work so hard reviewing our cases. Take a break, girl. They'll still be on your desk when you get back." Amina smiled.

Renee returned a half smile to her. "Thanks for the invite, but I really did bring my lunch. I'll eat it after a while."

"Okay, well, if you change your mind, just call me and I'll tell you where we are so you can come join us."

"Okay. And thanks for the invite."

Amina closed the door behind herself leaving Renee alone again with thoughts of Brandon and the what-ifs of her past plaguing her. She faced his file again and looked at the most recent notations in it. The date was marked the day before. The memory of her last visit with Brandon was all too fresh.

Two days before, she had received a call from a neighbor of the Miller's stating they hadn't seen Brandon traveling to school with the Miller's other foster kids over the past week. Renee contacted his school first and it was confirmed that he hadn't been to school in a week. Renee immediately left her office after ending her call with the school and headed over to the Miller's.

Since her office was allowed to make unannounced visits to families hosting foster kids, Renee didn't bother to call ahead and inform the Millers that she'd be paying them a visit.

She stood on their porch ringing the doorbell praying that she would keep her composure with the family if she found out that something bad had been going on with Brandon. She remembered his sad yet hopeful eyes the first time she met him. No child should have had to endure what Brandon had in such a short time, let alone in life ever. She rang the doorbell again only to look to her right and see someone peering at her through the window. She soon heard scrambling and muffled speech on the other side of the door.

In what seemed like forever, Mrs. Miller finally opened the door sporting pink sponge rollers in her head. She grunted and showcased a fake smile at Renee all at the same time. Because Renee had passed his case off to another social worker when she moved up the ranks, she hadn't been to the home since she'd drop Brandon off their four years earlier, which led to Mrs. Miller not remembering Renee's name. "I assume you're with DCFS?"

"Yes," Renee said adamantly. "I received notice that Brandon hadn't been to school in a week and I came to check up on the matter."

"Well, why ain't Roy come to investigate like he normally does when that nosey neighbor of mines runs her mouth?" She stuck her neck out of her door and screamed, "you old nosey heifer," hoping her neighbor would indeed hear her.

"Roy is out of the office on vacation." Renee's eyebrows wrinkled. "And what do you mean when he normally comes to investigate your neighbor's accusations? According to our records, Roy only comes for the routine visits, not because someone called on you."

Mrs. Miller's expression turned to one similar to a child caught cheating on a test. She cleared her throat before speaking again, "I just mean, Roy normally comes."

"May I come in?" Renee demanded more so than asked.

Mrs. Miller looked over her shoulder into her house as if she were checking to see if the coast was clear to allow Renee to enter.

Renee didn't even allow her to respond before she spoke again. "Mrs. Miller, need I remind you that we are permitted to make unannounced visits and you're required to comply."

"Well come on in then." Mrs. Miller lips curled into a snarl as she stepped to the side, allowing Renee to enter.

It was midday on a school day so Renee was surprised to walk in and see all five of the other foster children placed in the home practically standing in line by height. They smiled and nodded their heads at her. Renee looked around the first floor of the two story home to see large boxes spread everywhere. "Moving are you?" She stared at Mrs. Miller.

Mrs. Miller closed the front door chuckling. "Uh yeah, these kids are getting bigger, but this house ain't. We decided to move some place bigger."

"Well, you know you have to notify us of your plans to move."

"I know that." Mrs. Miller snapped at Renee. She slowly composed herself as she went and stood near the kids side-eyeing them. "We were just waiting until we secured everything before we called y'all."

"Well, I see all of the kids are here except for Brandon. And since I know he's not at school, where is he?"

All of the kids' heads dropped as if in shame.

Mrs. Miller stammered trying to speak, "Well, you see what happened was, he ran away."

"Ran away?" Renee's voice elevated.

"Yes. We've been looking everywhere for him and we haven't found him." Mrs. Miller whimpered.

Renee looked over at the kids all looking like submissive slaves to their master. It was as if Mrs.

25

Miller had coached them on how to act just before Renee came through the door.

Renee had enough of Mrs. Miller's shenanigans. She ordered the kids to make their way to the front door. She was taking them with her. Of course Mrs. Miller protested their removal and although Renee gave off a timid demeanor in most situations, she had the authority of a lion in a jungle defending its territory when it came to kids under her stead. Mrs. Miller's antics to keep the kids that day paled in comparison to Renee's determination to remove them since she was so leery of the Millers during the visit.

After taking the kids back to the office and coworkers helping to interview them, they all confessed to the Millers abusing them on the regular, verified by varying scars and wounds on each of them. They all recounted the same tale that the last time Mrs. Miller beat Brandon so bad, he ended up in the hospital.

After days of searching for him, Renee was able to locate Brandon in a hospital near the Miller's home where they anonymously left him unconscious in the hospital's care.

All in one day, the Millers were arrested on child abuse for all of the kids and attempted murder in the case of Brandon. The further she got into her investigation, she found out that Roy, the other worker assigned to the case, was Mr. Miller's cousin. He got a cut of the money the Millers received from the state per month from all six kids being with them if he would only look the other way when he came to visit the kids. Of course that led to him omitting the evidence of abuse from his reported visits.

It broke her heart seeing Brandon's thin body lying helpless in the hospital bed with tubes attached to almost every part of it. The doctor admitted to her that the possibility of him making a full recovery after receiving so many blows to his head was slim to none.

Renee sat at her desk as her tears began to soak the pages of his files. Her heart ached beyond just what Brandon had been through.

She sobbed wondering if the son she had given up for adoption when she was in college had suffered at the hands of his adoptive parents.

2

"Guess where I'm taking you all next weekend," Monica squealed as she stared into the faces of her best friends after she stuffed them with food. Monica had laid out a feast for them.

Kim normally went for seconds, but she didn't this time. Unfazed by Monica's question, she was too busy being grateful for the rest of the sisterhood not noticing her lack of eating. Or the fact that she wasn't eating her customary bag of chips as she sat on the floor.

Pam's toned frame reclined comfortably in the oversized chair in Monica's den. And of course, Renee sat to herself with the perfect mixture of curiosity and fear vexing her face.

They had attended the nine a.m. service at their church that morning. Now that they were full both spiritually and naturally, they planned to enjoy the rest of their Sunday together.

Kim finally decided to speak up, "Where?" She looked at Monica.

"Well, you all know that I plan events to everyone from city officials to bat mitzvahs." Monica chuckled. "Well, not too long ago, I was hired by Karen Roberts to plan her wedding to Kyle Irving."

Kim's face lit up with the knowledge of the names Monica dropped.

Pam and Renee were clueless as to who Monica was referring to and it showed in their aloof demeanor. Pam smiled while staring at the lock screen picture of her and her beau, Vance, while Renee absentmindedly played with the hem of her ankle length denim skirt.

Kim rose to her feet and strolled to sit next to Monica. "So, we get to go to their wedding with you in the city? Mmmh, since Kyle is an NBA star and Karen is a sports broadcaster, their guest list should be filled with fine, male celebrities who have yet to have the pleasure of meeting me." Her big, round, doe eyes sparkled with mischief as she puckered her full lips causing the dimples to deepen in her big cheeks. She blew them a kiss Marilyn Monroe style. "I think I've got just the right dress to turn heads that day."

Pam squinted her almond shaped eyes at Kim. "Everything is not about you."

"Oh whatever. You're off the market, I'm not. I can go up and down every aisle I want taste testing and picking out my meals based on my appetite at the moment." Kim smirked.

The rest of the sisterhood waited silently for Renee's response to Kim. She didn't speak. Where Renee would normally scold Kim for alluding to promiscuous behavior, her mind was lost in her past and she didn't even hear what Kim had said.

Kim galloped from her seat and jumped in Renee's face, flagging her attention with the wave of her hand. "Earth to Renee! Hello."

"Hunh?" Renee brought herself back to the current moment. She looked at everyone staring at her oddly. "What?"

"I pretty much announced my intentions to use my body to snag any man I want at the wedding," Kim's long eyelashes fluttered rapidly, "and yet you didn't have a condemning retort or quote a scripture to me." Kim raised her hands in a 'what's up with that' motion to Renee.

"Oh, I didn't hear you."

"What's up with you? You've been so quiet and withdrawn lately."

ANITA DAVIS

"I'm fine. I'm fine. Just thinking about a case with a little boy I've been involved in for a long time." *Try twelve years.*

"I guess, but that's why I tell you not to get so involved with those cases. They take a toll on your mental. You know I know that." Kim's perfectly glossed lips curled into a snarl. "I love my students, but I learned early on not to let their issues become my issues to the point where they cripple me. I can't be effective with them if I'm weighed down and hopeless like them. You were vibrant like me when we were growing up. I swear you haven't been the same since Ted in college."

Renee wrapped her arms tightly around herself at the mention of his name and where her troubles started.

Monica shot Kim an incredulous stare and mouthed to her, "Why'd you mention him?"

Kim shrugged her shoulders and slowly moved away from Renee. She knew she needed to shift the conversation from Ted to something or someone else immediately. She walked towards Pam. "And on to you, Missy. One minute you're cutting your hair, confessing that you had an affair with a married man, and then the next, you end up with our boss, Vance. Which leads me to believe he's the reason for that

31

ever present smile on your face and extra pep in your step."

Pam smiled, exposing all of her teeth. "Kim, stop being your meddling self with us right now. Yes, Vance makes me happy and it shows on my face, but you know this joy that I have comes from God."

Kim's big eyes slowly rolled to the back of her head as she inhaled a deep breath and her nostrils flared.

Pam ignored Kim's antics and continued on. "Maybe if you slowed down and took the time to get to know one guy, you'd fall in love and have an ever present smile on your face from one man rather than a fleeting one from one guy to the next. What's up with you and Darius anyway?"

Kim shook her head. "Oh you slay me." She regally placed her flat palm on her chest. "You all know that I'm not the relationship type. I will never fall in love with a man. So get over that notion and keep it moving. And he and I are still cool and kick it from time to time, but like I said, I'm not the relationship type."

They all laughed at Kim's theatrics except for Renee who was lost in thought yet again. She wasn't privy to anything that had been said since Kim had brought up Ted.

Kim turned to face Monica. "And of course we know where your endless joy stems from—my brother, your husband, Keith, and my beautiful twin niece and nephew."

Monica batted her eyes and licked her lips.

"Don't start that TMI mess with me about my brother. We don't want to know what you all do behind closed doors. Right, Renee?" Kim looked over to her sister, Renee, who normally agreed with her about Monica not needing to fill them in on her sexual exploits with their triplet brother, Keith, but Kim noted the far off look in Renee's eyes again and dared not pull her out of her trance. She feared that Renee might still be dwelling on her past with Ted. Even though she didn't want Renee thinking about that loser, she decided to leave Renee alone for the time being. She didn't want Renee to retreat into her shell even more if she pushed her too hard.

"Oh, whatever. You and Renee should be used to me doting on my husband by now. If he were any other man, you would be probing me to spill the beans on our love life, but because he's your brother, that topic is off limits? Nope, it might be for you, but because the marriage bed is not defiled, I'm not ashamed to share. Besides, it's not like I ever give details on how good it is." Monica laughed and stared at Kim who pretended to make herself gag. "Anyway, we started this conversation off with the fact that I would love for you ladies to join me in Aruba for Karen and Kyle's wedding."

Pam and Kim gasped with merriment while Renee still remained detached from what was going on around her.

"Aruba? They invited us?" Pam was in a bit of shock given Karen and Kyle didn't know any of them other than Monica.

"So do we have to pay for our airfare and hotel rooms?" Kim tilted her head to the side and her eyelids blinked rapidly as she stared at Monica.

"No. of course not. But if you all did, you could afford it."

"So what if we could? Doesn't mean we would want to spend our money on such a trip, but sense it's free, I'm definitely game." Kim finally made her way back to her spot on the floor and plopped down on the pillows she used as her makeshift seat.

"That's so nice of them. But why would they offer to pay for us?" Renee finally tuned in to the conversation.

"Welcome back from the dead, Lazarus." Kim stared at Renee.

"Leave her alone, Kim." Monica shook her head, trying to contain her laughter. "Well, whenever Karen and I talked while we were planning the wedding, I always managed to bring you all up at some point and how close we all are. You know, the sisterhood between us. She has a best friend that's dear to her, too, and since she'll be moving from here to Miami after the wedding and leaving her best friend here, she wanted my friends to come to the island with me so that we can create yet another memory to bond over as her and her friend, Melanie, have done countless times."

"Aww, that's so sweet of her," Pam said.

"Yeah, it is, but knowing that we'll be on an island now means that I have to change my outfit that I was going to wear to the wedding. Shoot, we're going away for the weekend? I need to update my wardrobe." Kim jumped up from the floor in search of her shoes.

"Now you know you have enough clothes in your closet suitable for any destination on this earth," Monica said, watching Kim's rapid movements.

"Yeah, but I know for certain there will be professional athletes there so I have to spice up my outfits a bit," Kim said.

"Okay, ladies. So you all are down to go to Aruba with me next weekend?"

They all nodded their heads in agreement.

"Great, so let's talk business."

Kim snapped her head back at Monica as she was halfway to the front door. "Business? What business? This will be a pleasure trip for me."

"Kim, although you can have fun while you're there, which I'm *sure* you will, I will need you all's help to make sure that everything goes the way it should for the wedding." Monica's eyes pleaded with each of them for their support.

Pam smiled and nodded her agreement.

Renee gave a half smile as she drew her knees in to her chin.

"Good, I'm certain between the three of you all, the wedding will flow without a hiccup." Kim's naturally pouty lips curved up feigning a smile.

"Three of us? So you won't go? You won't help?" Monica walked over to the doorway to stare Kim eye to eye.

"Oh no, I'm going, I just won't be helping with the wedding, I'll find a lucky man to serve some of my helpings to." And on that note Kim headed to the front door.

"Where are you going?" Monica called out to her.

"To get my servings in order." She laughed and waved over her shoulder before closing the door behind her.

Monica walked back into the den where Pam and Renee still sat. She looked over at Pam who was smiling, lost in thought. She could tell from the gleam in Pam's eyes that she must've been thinking about Vance, but when she looked over at Renee, she wasn't aware of what had Renee in such gloom and despair.

Monica made the hissing sound to Pam and then nodded her head in Renee's direction.

Picking up on what she thought Monica was hinting at, Pam got up from her seat and walked the short distance with Monica over to Renee. Pam joined Renee in the oversized seat and Monica squatted in front of them.

"Renee, what's wrong, sweetie?" Pam asked.

It took a moment for it to register where she was and who was speaking to her. When she finally did stare into the faces of her friends, she worked hard to hold back the tears trying to escape her eyes. She knew if she stayed there any longer, out would come the skeleton in her closet.

She still hadn't fully digested the resurgence of the emotions that had been taunting her since Brandon's file had reappeared on her desk. She knew she wasn't ready to share with the sisterhood what was going on with her, no matter how close they were. "Nothing." Her voice trembled as she jumped from her seat and rushed out of the house to her car.

Pam and Monica ran after her. "Renee, come back." They stood in the doorway, no longer seeing

Renee's taillights. They looked at each other, and Monica spoke up, "First it was me that needed an intervention, then it was you, and now it seems like we have to get to the bottom of whatever is troubling Renee." she sighed.

"Yeah, but sadly like Kim said earlier, Renee hasn't been the same since Ted. I think getting her to open about whatever is going on with her is going to be a lot more work than it took for you and I."

3

It was the day before the wedding and Monica sat next to Pam with their toes in the sand, starring out into the clear blue waters. "I wish she would come over here and sit with us," Pam whispered.

Monica directed her attention to Renee who sat at least one-hundred feet away from them further down the shore.

"Well at least she came at all. Think about how much we called her this past week and she didn't return our calls or answer the door when we stopped by her place."

"You're right. I was shocked when she walked onto the plane."

Pam laughed. "Yeah. Thank God that Kim is as bold and brazen as she is and literally dragged Renee out of her house."

"Yeah, her feistiness definitely benefitted us this go round. I just wish that Renee would open up to us about whatever has had her so withdrawn from us for a while," Monica said.

"Me, too, but just like you and I, light bulbs had to click in our heads before we finally decided to open up to the rest of the sisterhood."

"Renee is just different. As bold as she is with her prayers and quoting scriptures on the regular, it must really be something heavy going on for her to withdraw like this," Monica said.

Pam sighed as Kim sashayed up to them. As she probably intended, the black netted sarong Kim wore to cover up her string leopard bikini left little to the imagination. She shimmied in front of Pam and Monica.

"Ladies, look where we are." She twirled with her hands wide. Her rich, sun kissed skin, full lips, and doe eyes made her look like a native Aruban rather than a visitor for the weekend. "No need to sit next to each other, let's move around. Mingle with the natives and have some fun."

Monica held up the ring finger on her left hand. "I know what your definition of mingling is. Need I remind you that I'm a happily married woman?" She looked to Pam while nudging her. "And this here love stricken woman is pretty much at the altar herself, so there will be no mingling for either of us."

Kim dropped in the sand and crossed her legs in front of her. "Yeah whatever. I don't 'mingle' with every man I meet. I meant let's flirt and have a little fun while we're here."

"Flirt? I told you I'm married." Monica bucked her dark brown eyes at Kim.

"I can understand you, Monica. In fact, you better not cheat on my brother, but until Vance puts a ring on Pam's finger, pays for the wedding, and they say, 'I do,' she can flirt."

Monica swatted at Kim trying to brush off how silly Kim could be at times.

Pam cleared her throat and focused her stare on Kim. "You're right, I can flirt if I want to, but the key thing is if I want to. I don't. Vance is all the man I need." She smiled.

Kim scrunched her face up. "Ugh, love is so overrated."

"No it isn't." Pam shot back quick like a kindergartener arguing with one of their classmates. "What's up with you and Darius? You two seemed to hit it off at our school's picnic at the end of the summer. No budding relationship there?"

"No. I just told you last week that he and I are cool." Kim smiled. "Darius is the male version of

Untold

me." She laughed. "He gets me. We spend *time* together, but he doesn't want anything serious either, so that makes him a great go-to guy."

Monica shook her head. "I don't know where you get such a blasé attitude with your body. You weren't like this when we were growing up, and I know your momma didn't raise you to be a hussy."

Kim's eyes widened in shock of Monica's choice words for her. "I am not a hussy. I'm just a liberated woman who knows what she wants and conducts herself as such."

"Alright now, keep it up and you'll end up with something you can't get rid of, if you know what I mean." Monica gave Kim the side eye.

Kim let her mouth gape wide open as she draped her hand across her chest feigning disappointment in Monica. "You all must really think I share my cookie with everyone."

Monica and Pam turned their heads away from Kim and pretended as if something else was calling their attention.

Kim reached out and slapped Pam and Monica on their knees. They laughed, turning back to face her.

"Well that's the impression you give, always hinting at who you're about to bed and the seductive ways you talk about your male suitors," Pam said.

"I admit that I've been with quite a few men, but it's not like I'm with a different one every night, every week. I just don't want a relationship and so when I get the urge and I want my needs met, there is always a man I can call on, but it's generally the same man until he either gets to clingy or jumps into a relationship with someone else and I have to find another suitor." She stared at them with a straight face as if her explanation would satisfy them and end the discussion there.

"If you say so, but we all grew up with the same morals, so something triggered your liberation into giving your body to someone other than your husband, not to mention the odd thing you have against relationships." Monica stared into Kim's bright eyes.

"Oh enough about me. What about that sister of mine?"

They all looked down the shore at Renee sitting by herself.

The sounds of the waves and music blaring in the distance from a nearby midday pool party at the resort accompanied them as they stood and headed toward Renee who was constantly wiping at her face as if she were trying to free it of tears.

4

Renee stood in the back and away from the rest of the crowd as she waited for the bride to make her way down the sandy path to her groom. She was grateful that the women didn't push her the day before to confess to them why she cried as she sat on the beach. They had become so consumed with helping Monica with the last minute to do list for the wedding that they didn't have time to interrogate her anymore. She just hoped that she would be as fortunate to make it back home without them bombarding her with questions as to why she was so gloomy.

She looked up to see the groom constantly looking over his shoulder and she knew just why. Monica had shared with them the night before that the groom's best man and close friend, Andrew, hadn't shown up for the wedding yet and Kyle and Karen weren't sure if he would at all.

Soft music began to play, signaling that the bride would soon make her appearance. Renee looked to where Monica stood and knew she was readying the bride to make her grand entrance, but a quiet commotion near the groom pulled her attention in his direction. She saw a man—a tall, deeply sun kissed, handsome one at that—out of breath, run up to Kyle and pat him on his back. When she saw the smile on Kyle's face and his shoulders relax, she reasoned the man wearing a similar linen suit as Kyle must be his estranged best man.

She heard the oohs and aahs of everyone near her and she knew that the bride was making her way down the path laid out for her that would lead to her groom, but she couldn't manage to pull her attention from the best man. There was something about him that drew her to him. Her gaze was so fixated on him that she didn't even notice that he was staring back at her. When her dark brown eyes finally locked with his, the bitterness in his made her turn away from him. How could she be drawn to him and yet feel sad for him at the same time? There was a quickening in her spirit and she knew that meant that God had called her to pray for him. She looked up to the sky and mumbled,

"God, You already know what I'm dealing with. Why would you give me someone else to pray for?"

She had been crying a lot lately over Brandon and the skeleton in her closet that she might have to soon dig up, but that didn't stop her from interceding on Brandon's behalf and seeking God for what to do with her personal matter. She spent a lot of time before God for those two issues. She knew adding this man, this breathtaking man that her eyes kept locking on, would require even more of her time to lay before God and pray for, not that she had a problem with being in His presence though.

Even with distance between them, she could sense the heaviness he was carrying and she could feel that whatever was troubling him was just as weighty as her burden. It showed in the downtrodden look in his eyes and the slumped shoulders of his posture. She finally pulled her attention from him to look at the bride. She smiled briefly reveling in how stunning Karen looked in her designer gown as she stood next to her groom. The radiant and vibrant hues of the sun setting over the blue waters was the ultimate fantasy backdrop for nuptials.

Renee stood still as the soft summer breeze and the waves washing ashore serenaded her while the couple exchanged their vows. She didn't know how long she stood there, but soon, she felt a pulling on her arm.

"Renee, Renee. Come on, let's go."

"Hunh?" Renee pulled herself into the moment and focused her attention on the person that was guiding her. "Where are we going?" Renee spoke to Pam.

Although they weren't the same height, Pam's shorter stature locked arms with Renee and guided their path. "Well, had you been paying attention, you would've heard Monica instructing the guests where to go for the candlelight reception."

Renee looked around the sands where the small group of guests for the wedding once stood. It was now empty except for workers from the hotel removing the arch and the few chairs allocated for guests who couldn't manage to stand during the ceremony.

"Come on, Renee." Pam pulled Renee as they entered the dimly lit dining area beautifully decorated with flowers indigenous to the island.

Pam kept her elbow locked with Renee's as she scanned the tables for their name settings. She found it quickly and sat down at the table forcing Renee to sit next to her. "Renee." She squeezed Renee's hand. "It's clear to us that you're dealing with something that you're not ready to share with us just yet. On one hand, I know how it feels to have people prying in your life when you just want to be left alone. But had you all not pried into mine when I was in despair and condemning myself, especially you with all of the praying and interceding you did for me," Pam smiled at Renee, "I wouldn't be sane and sitting here right now with you. We're giving you some time sweetie to deal with whatever it is that you're dealing with, but just know that we're here for you whenever you're ready to open up to us. And remember that we won't let you wallow for too long before we force your truth out of you."

Renee raised one of her hardly arched eyebrows at Pam.

Pam chuckled. "I don't care how you look at me. I mean, you really have been out of it today. Had I not dragged you in here, you probably would've still been out there all alone staring off into the now dark skies. I need you to at least be aware of your surroundings while you're here and not so lost in thought."

"You're right." Renee gave Pam a half smile before she looked past Pam and locked eyes with the best man, Andrew. He seemed as sad as her. She reasoned that the groom must be a good friend of his. She could see that Kyle was just as concerned about him as the sisterhood was about her because rushed him off by the arm, just like Pam did her earlier.

***

"You know I should ring your neck for barely making it to my wedding, but I'll give you a pass since I know what you're going through. How are you?" Kyle stood against a wall in the hallway outside of the dining area where the reception was being held. He knew he should be sitting next to his new wife and enjoying the guests that came to celebrate the day with them, but after all, Karen had encouraged him to check up on his best friend.

He hadn't been able to reach Andrew since he went missing after the news his birth mother dealt him about his real father. He was glad that Andrew had at least listened to his messages to know where the wedding would be and that he actually showed up.

Andrew leaned against the wall opposite of Kyle. He rubbed the five o'clock shadow on his face. His eyes were red as if he hadn't slept in days and his normally low cut hair had grown out into a mini afro. "I guess as good as I can be given what I know now."

"So you still haven't talked to him yet?"

"No."

"Why not? If he did rape your birth mother, Marie, there's no excuse for it, but you should talk to him. Hear his side of the story and then figure out how you'll interact with him from there."

Andrew pushed himself from off the wall with the sole of his foot and walked over to be face to face with Kyle. "I looked into Marie's eyes when she confessed to me that my father raped her, and I believe her. The man that raised me, took me to all of my basketball games, taught me how to shave, schooled me on women, never let me slack up on school, is a liar."

The man who adopted me when I was four years old raped my mother." Andrew fazed out for a moment as if his statement was a fresh epiphany for him. "He's the reason why she gave me up in the first place. He's kept me wondering where I really came from all of these years. I've been wondering about my birth parents for so long. Why they gave me up for adoption? If they had other kids, when in reality, I was living with my real father and my real sister and brother all along. What am I supposed to say to him? Thanks, Dad. Thanks for raping my mother and somehow miraculously adopting me years later. Thanks for being in my life and being that father figure for me even though you really were my father all along. Is that what I'm supposed to say to him? Hunh?" Andrew stared at Kyle.

"I don't know, I just know you need to say something to him. Everyone is worried about you. Thank God Marie and Melanie are here because now they know that you are okay. But your adopted mom, brother, and sister have been calling me, trying to see if I knew where you had disappeared too. At least call them and let them know that you're okay."

"You mean my blood brother and sister?"

"Yeah, I guess they are your blood siblings. So that's all the more reason to call them and tell them you're okay."

"I can't do that."

"And why not?" Kyle's face scrunched in confusion.

"Because then I run the risk of him answering the phone. I can't guarantee what I would say to him if I talked to him or saw him right now."

"Well then just call the others on their cell phones and let them know. Text them or something."

"You know how close we all are. It's best if I say nothing for now. It won't stop at a hello with them. They'll keep going until they learn why I've been avoiding them."

"But that's not a bad thing. Just deal with this situation head on and let the chips fall where they may."

Andrew rubbed the creases in his creamy dark brown forehead as he sighed. "Look, this is your day. It's not about me. Sorry I was late getting here. I

51

honestly didn't know if I was even going to show up, but I just couldn't let you down on your big day."

"Thanks, I appreciate it." Kyle gripped Andrew's extended hand and held on to it as they patted each other on the back in a brotherly embrace.

"Now let's get you back in there to that beautiful bride of yours." Andrew mustered up a smile.

"I know, right? I'm certain she's looking for me by now."

Just as Kyle and Andrew were headed back into the dining area, Marie and Melanie came out in search of him.

Kyle looked over to Andrew. "I'll catch you later."

"Alright." Andrew sighed and lowered his head awaiting Marie and Melanie's interrogation of him.

"Drew. My baby. Where have you been?" Marie's raspy voice trembled as she wrapped her arms around him and squeezed him as hard as she could. She could only imagine what he was going through and she wanted her embrace to impart as much love as it could into him.

His shoulders finally relaxed as he allowed Marie's hug to fully engulf him. He sniffed to keep the tears welling in his eyes from falling. For as long as he had known that he was an adopted child, he always wanted to know his birth mom—her touch, her voice, the gleam in her eyes whenever she saw him. He was grateful that he had finally found Marie. Ever since they first reconnected, he felt her love for him, and he definitely felt the depth of her love for him in the hug she was giving him. However, he despised the reason why she was hugging him so tightly. He knew she had been raped and conceived him and could not keep him because he reminded her so much of the man that raped her. After months of him begging her to tell him who his birth father was, she saw a picture of his adoptive father holding his newborn niece and it shook her to her core. Andrew saw her reaction and pressed her to tell him why she had become so irate when she saw it.

Ready to move on past that part of her life since it had held her in mental bondage for a long time, she confessed to him that his adoptive father was actually his biological father, the man who had raped her. With that revelation, Andrew had ran off, leaving Marie and everyone else who cared about him worried about him and his whereabouts.

Marie pulled back from him to stare him in his face. She kissed both of his cheeks and then stared at him again. "My God, what have I done to my children?"

Melanie came closer to the duo as she spoke. "Mom, what are you talking about? You didn't do anything."

"Yes I did. You looked just as ghastly last year as he does now after you found out that he was your brother when he spotted me at Karen's almost wedding to that con artist, Dennis."

Their initial reunion at the wedding was just like a scene in a movie. Andrew saw Marie first and remembered looking into those eyes of hers until he was four years old. Marie knew he was the son she had given up for adoption because he looked just like the man that had raped her back when she was in college. They broke the news to Melanie that her then boyfriend Andrew was actually her brother. She threw up. Although completely disturbing to Melanie that she had dated, kissed her brother, she was grateful that they never had sex.

While Melanie still struggled at times to get past her disdain for not knowing that she dated her blood brother, Andrew handled the situation differently. He was too busy focusing on reconnecting with the birth mother he longed for all of his life rather than dwelling on having dated his blood sister. Melanie had avoided him and Marie for a few months and when she did get back around him, he visibly saw her shudder when people either brought up the fact that they once dated or that they were brother and sister.

Andrew looked over at Melanie and waited for her to shiver in disgust as she did whenever she was reminded that she had dated him not knowing that he was her biological brother. Andrew smiled before speaking. "You didn't shake when she said that. I guess it doesn't gross you out any more."

"Oh no, it still does when I think about it. But you know I knew deep down that neither of us knew that we were siblings when we fell in love. I'm just glad that things didn't go too far before we found out the truth. But enough about that." She pulled at the curls in his 'fro, uncomfortable with rehashing her time with him as his girlfriend. "Mom's right. You look bad. What are you trying to do, grow a natural like mine?" She laughed, trying to lighten up the mood.

"I haven't been concerned about the way I look. I'm more concerned about these raging feelings of mine." Andrew pulled back from Marie with fire in his eyes. "I wanna believe you, Mom." He looked into her eyes. "I do believe you that my dad… Charles did to you what you said he did. It just doesn't make sense to me." Andrew rubbed his hands through the tight curls on his head before he rested his back against the nearby wall.

Marie rushed to him and pulled his hands from his head and gripped them in hers. "I'm sorry, sweetie. This is all my fault. If I hadn't given you up for adoption, you wouldn't have even met him. You wouldn't be in the turmoil that you're in now." She reached out and pulled him into another one of her warm embraces.

"Ma." Andrew tried to pull back from Marie, but her grip was too tight on him. He smiled and finally relaxed his body in her grasp and allowed his arms to drop to his sides.

She hesitantly pulled back from him. "I'm sorry for smothering you, but you just don't know how I've felt not knowing how you've been since I told you who he was. It's almost been as worse as it was for all of those years I wondered where you were and who had you," Marie cried out. "That monster."

Melanie's tall, yet slender, Hershey's Kiss coated frame draped in her flowing maid of honor gown, went to her mother's side and rubbed her back. She leaned her head on her shoulder.

"Don't cry, Ma." Andrew wiped at the tears on Marie's face.

Just then Renee stepped out of the dining area headed to the bathroom. She locked eyes with Andrew's tight alluring eyes and had to pry herself from the trance he held her in to continue to the bathroom.

Andrew shook his head trying to refocus his thoughts on the people in front of him. He looked at Marie. "You didn't hurt you. He did. Although I hate that you gave me up, I can see how you felt that was your only choice at the time." He wiped away more of Marie's ever falling tears. "Look, I didn't mean to make this day, this moment for Kyle and Karen, about me. Just go back in there and try to enjoy yourselves."

"What about you?" Melanie asked with worry in her voice.

"I don't know, Mel. I don't know what I'm gonna do." Andrew sighed as Melanie squeezed his hand in support of him. Marie kissed his cheek one last time before heading back to the dining area.

Andrew rubbed his face and shook his head at the noise his hairy face made. He looked down at what he wore and knew that if Karen hadn't left the white linen suit at the front desk for him, he'd really look terrible. He would've staggered onto the sand for the wedding wearing the jogging pants and T-shirt he donned on the plane ride to the island.

The day had become more about him than Karen and Kyle and he knew he needed to fix that. He lifted himself off the wall and headed to the bathroom to give himself a once over in the mirror and hoped he didn't look as bad as everyone had made him out to look. He knew he hadn't shaved or gotten a haircut since he left Marie's house weeks ago, but he hoped his strong jawline and smooth, chocolate skin was balancing out his scruffiness.

As of late, he walked with his head low and made his way down the hallway. The only things he could hear were the meddling thoughts in his head and the loud shuffling of footsteps on the tiled floor nearing him.

He slowly lifted his head to see who was walking towards him and made eye contact with those same beautiful, deep brown eyes that had temporarily suspended the misery he was drowning in when he walked up to Kyle earlier during the ceremony. He was grateful for her presence because she gave his emotions a reprieve from his troubles. And again, he found himself thankful to be in her presence in the hallway staring into her captivating eyes.

His cares seemed to detach from him, leaving him to see the despair in hers. He didn't know her but he wished that he could fix whatever was troubling her. He wanted to be able to see the sparkle in her eyes he bet was brilliant if only she wasn't as weighed down as she seemed.

Neither of them said anything as they gazed into one another's eyes and for just that moment he was in complete peace.

Renee slowly peeled her eyes away from his and made her way back to the reception.

Andrew hated that he was staring at her walking away rather than into her eyes because now menacing thoughts of what he would do or say to his father the next time he saw him plagued him once again.

5

The alarm clock buzzed signaling Renee that morning had arrived. She yawned and stretched causing her lavender cover to crumple in her lap. She slowly opened her eyes trying to adjust them to the darkness in the room. She could tell from the scattered rays of sun peeking from behind her drapes that the sun was out in all of its glory, but her sun blocking drapes prevented the sunlight from shining into the room as brightly as it was on the other side of them.

As a part of her morning ritual, she arose from her bed and opened the curtains. She thought letting the sunlight into the darkness of her bedroom mirrored how she welcomed God to shine light on any dark area in her life daily. She needed Him to do just that at this juncture in her life. She had been praying for Brandon's healing and to recover from his brain trauma but he still hadn't awoke from his comma.

And then there was her son that she didn't know what to do about. As much as she wanted God to give her clarity about which way to go with the issue, her fear of what she would uncover stifled her. Not to mention the burden she had been experiencing to pray for the man she managed to lock eyes with a few times while she was on the island. She just didn't know what to pray for him, but that didn't matter to her because her prayers were rarely in English anyway.

The light beamed in the room as she pressed play on her iPod. Shekinah Glory's worship album filled the room with a stirring melody.

Despite the turmoil she felt over her secret, she didn't let it hinder her interceding on behalf of others and crying out to God. "Hallelujah. Thank You, Jesus. Bless Your name, God." She paced the floor near her bed with outstretched hands. "Glory to Your name, God. You're worthy. You're awesome, God. You're mighty. You're powerful, God." Her voice trembled as she praised God. She wouldn't let the praise of those on the song out do her praise to her God.

There was a quickening in her spirit, and she bent over with open arms as her words shifted to another language.

She fell to her knees under the weight of the Holy Ghost and prayed in tongues for about ten minutes before she fell silent on carpeted floor and basked in the presence of God. She stood to her feet and wiped her face dry of her tears of reverence to God. "I thank You, God, that Brandon is healed by the blood of the lamb and the resurrected power of Your son, Jesus. And I thank You, God, that the man with those gorgeous yet down trodden eyes would seek You where You may be found. That he would cry out to You and receive You as his own. Lord, please lift the burden from him and fix whatever is wrong in his life. In Your dear son Jesus' name, amen." Renee smiled knowing God would heal Brandon and that He could encourage the handsome stranger.

She headed to her bathroom to ready herself for work, and when she looked in the mirror at how tired she looked from having cried herself to sleep yet another night, tears fell from her eyes. She wondered if she would ever free herself from the guilt of her past.

***

Renee trotted into work mumbling affirmations of positivity to herself. With the cases that she dealt with of misplaced and abused kids, she couldn't afford to have her personal issues weigh her down any more than her workload did.

She smiled at her coworkers as she walked past them and let out a loud sigh of relief when she finally closed her office door behind her. She had managed to escape them without any questions of why she looked as tired as she did. She didn't wear makeup, but after looking at herself in the mirror that morning, she put on foundation, concealer, and mascara hoping to make herself look rejuvenated and kempt. But those pesky lines and bags seemed to have permanently etched themselves around and under her eyes.

She planned to take advantage of her duties as a supervisor and not have to leave her office. She wasn't sure she could take going into the homes of any of the kids in the cases on her desk. *But I will stop by and see Brandon after work. No one that I know of visits him and prays for him.*

She sat at her desk and pressed the play button on her iPod. Again, worship music surrounded her and she hoped it would balance out the negative energy from the actions of her past. She sifted through the cases on her desk making sure that her juniors were staying on top of their caseloads or as close to it as possible. She shook her head thinking how ironic it was that she believed God to heal, bless, and provide peace to others, yet she couldn't tap into and gain total peace for herself. She wouldn't stop trying though.

An hour into sorting through the files on her desktop of resolved cases versus pending investigations, she came across one that stumped her breathing. She had seen Phillip's file often within the last year. He kept being returned to the agency by every foster home they had placed him in. She shook her head in sadness. It wasn't Phillip's fault that his mother wasn't attentive to him when he was a toddler and let him eat pencils and paint thus the varying symptoms he displayed of lead poisoning. As adorable as he was, the attention he now required was too much for many to handle. They had to be especially careful with who they placed him with since he would never be able to articulate if he was being abused or not. And sadly enough, he had to be removed from two of the homes he was placed in because his mouth didn't say it, but his body told that he had indeed been physically abused.

Renee cringed remembering the open wounds she saw on his back after a neighbor reported the piercing screams he heard coming from the apartment of the couple Phillip was placed with. Although she didn't have to, Renee determined that she would personally see over his case from that day forward.

It was now after lunch and Renee had avoided going out to eat with her coworkers yet again. She ate the lean cuisine she had brought from home and studied her daily devotional during lunch. As much as she tried to blot out her past and what she had done, the constant images of Brandon and Phillip being abused and abandoned played over and over in her head. The footage made her wonder, mortified, if her son had endured any of what they had experienced. Granted she saw happy endings to the permanent placement of many of the children that came through the agency, but it was those horrifying cases that resurrected thoughts of her son and how he was doing in life at the moment.

Phillip's case pricked her heart and further plagued that gnawing curiosity of hers about her son's well-being.

Is this You, God, urging me to seek him out? She thought. She had been praying that God would take away the desire for her to learn where her son was since she gave him up, even though she felt she had a good reason to do so at the time. But since the urge wasn't going away and only getting stronger, she knew she had to find him and soon. She realized that God wouldn't give her peace about the situation until she was obedient and did as He said. She just hoped she heard Him correctly.

6

"It smells so good in here. I know just what I want." Monica smiled as she put her menu down. "Ladies, wasn't Aruba beautiful?"

"Yeah, it was aiight." Kim sipped on her Pina colada.

"You were on a beautiful island witnessing one of the most romantic weddings I have ever seen. Why the sour response, Kim?" Pam placed her menu on the table as well.

"Because, when Monica told me who was getting married, I thought I would be able to garner the attention of several pro ball players. I guess they took the idea of an intimate wedding to the extreme. Hardly anyone was there. And the only players that did show up brought their wives with them." She took a sip of her drink and peered over the glass big rim before speaking again. "I may be into casual sex with the appointed man here and there, but I don't do married men. I have more sense than that."

Everyone was eerily quiet at the table and it soon hit Kim why no one had responded to her declaration. She looked up at Pam who was rubbing the frost off her glass of iced tea. "I'm sorry, Pam." She reached over to pat Pam's hand as she continued apologizing to her. "I wasn't saying you didn't have any sense, I was just, I—"

"No need to apologize." Pam squeezed Kim's hand in comfort. "You're right. I didn't have enough sense at the time to stop myself from dealing with Steve after I learned he was married. But thank God I did finally come to my senses and left him alone."

"Yes. Thank God," Monica chimed in.

Kim tilted her head to the side staring at Renee. "What, no quoting scriptures from you thus far? I brought up my fornicating ways and Pam rehashed her affair with a married man and you say nothing about the ways of a virtuous woman and living right for God? What's up with you, Renee? Renee?"

Renee snapped out of her catatonic like state after the second time Kim called her name. "Hunh?" Her hairy eyebrows raised in confusion.

People chattered at nearby tables and silverware clanked against plates as the ladies stared at Renee.

She was seemingly slipping back into her dismal trance.

Renee received a reprieve from a full-on interrogation from the ladies when the waiter came to take their order. Monica, Pam, and Kim placed their orders and then the waiter directed his attention to Renee. "And what will you have?"

"Renee." Kim nudged her to speak.

Renee barely looked up at him as she spoke. "Oh, I'll have what she's having." She pointed to Kim.

"Okay, ladies. Your food should be ready in no time." He left the table leaving the hawk eyes of the ladies staring down on Renee.

Kim angled her body completely towards Renee. "Renee Katrina Williams. What is up with you? Even though you've been around us physically since I forced you to, you've been so distant mentally. And that food you just ordered, we're fraternal triplets for a reason, we're nothing alike. And certainly when it comes to food. Although I keep my body up, you still get on me for not putting the best food choices in it." *Although I should know better.* Kim quieted her inner thoughts refusing to focus on her ongoing issue and put her attention back on her sister. "What the heck is up with you? You're starting to worry me."

"All of us," Monica said.

Pam nodded her head in agreement.

Renee racked her brain trying to figure out what she could say to get them off her back. "It's these cases you all, they..." Her words trailed off as she locked eyes with the handsome stranger she met on the island and had been praying for.

***

"Andrew. Andrew?" Kyle called out.

"Hunh?"

"You brought me here to celebrate my move to Miami, but you ain't celebrating. And what keeps getting your attention over there?" Kyle turned his head in the direction Andrew had been focused on since they sat at their table. He smiled. "Oh, a who. A woman. Gon' playa. It's time for you to get back in the game."

Andrew only heard fragments of what Kyle was saying. "Playa? Game? I'm not into her like that. She just looks familiar."

"Well, I'm just glad you getting your flow back. I know you still haven't figured out what you'll do with your dad, but at least you're back to dealing with your clients, especially me. Although I won't be playing ball anymore, there are still a lot of other deals I'll need you to run point on for me."

"For sure." Andrew gave Kyle a fist bump as he allowed his gaze to settle again on the woman across the restaurant, although she was no longer looking at him.

Kyle looked back over his shoulder again. "You say you ain't into her, but your eyes say otherwise." Kyle squinted trying to get a better look at the woman Andrew couldn't keep his eyes off when he spotted Monica.

Andrew pulled his eyes away from Renee to see Kyle leaving the table. "Where are you going?"

"Over there to say hi," Kyle responded.

"Why?" Andrew's eyebrows knitted together in confusion.

Kyle laughed. "Because I see the woman who made me and Karen's special day on the island possible." He looked at Andrew still vexed by his decision to go to the table full of women. "Bro, chill. I ain't gon' blow your cover with the woman you can't keep your eyes off of. I'm simply going over to say hi and again thank Monica for her work." Kyle smirked and shook his head as he walked off.

Andrew wiped his forehead before letting it drop in his locked hands on the table.

Kyle finally made his way over to the table and stood near Monica. "Excuse me, ladies, I hate to interrupt your evening, but I just had to come over when I saw you, Monica. Thank you again for everything that you did to make me and Karen's wedding as special as you did." He smiled and stretched his arms out wide.

Monica stood up from the table to give him a brotherly hug. "No problem. It was my pleasure." She let him go but still stood face to face with him. "I merely executed Karen's vision for the day." Monica faced the table. "Kyle, let me introduce you to my friends since I didn't get the opportunity to do so at the wedding. This is Pam." Pam shook his extended hand. "And this is Renee."

"Hello." Renee smiled as best as she could and grip his outstretched hand.

"And this is Kim."

Kim gripped his hand firmly and held on to it as she spoke. "Hello. Your wedding was beautiful, however, I must admit I was a little," she held up her other hand as if pinching something in the air, "disappointed to not see any single basketball players there. I was looking forward to mingling with them."

Monica shot Kim an incredulous look while Pam lowered her head and shook it. Renee had fallen back into a trance and was oblivious to Kim's crassness at the time.

"Please excuse my friend, she's just—"

"Being herself." Kyle laughed. "That's okay. I married a woman who is very vocal. It's cool. Anyway ladies, sorry to interrupt your evening, I'll get back over to my table since I see my food just arrived, and oh, here is yours." Kyle stepped aside to allow the server to place the entrees in front of each of the ladies.

"Okay. Enjoy your meal," Monica said.

"Bye, Kyle," Pam and Kim managed to say at the same time.

Monica took her seat. "Okay let's say grace and eat." She held her hands out signaling to the other ladies that they should all join hands. Everyone obliged except Renee.

"Renee!" Kim stared at Renee as she stared away from the table. Kim reached over and pinched her.

"Ouch. Why'd you do that?" Renee looked to Kim in confusion.

"Because the food is here and we've been holding our hands out for forever waiting for you to take them so we can pray. In all of that, you haven't paid us any mind. What is up with you? Say grace so we can drill you to see why you've become such a hermit."

Renee grabbed Kim and Pam's hands and bowed her head. "Lord God, we thank You for this food we're about to eat, and we thank You for the hands that prepared it. In Jesus' name. Amen."

They all stared at her as she picked up her fork and mindlessly poked at the food on her plate. She somehow felt their stares and looked up. "What?" Her airy voice was just above whisper level.

"You're the what. No long-winded prayers for us? No praying for the nations?" Kim shook her head in amazement.

"I still pray like that, just now right now."

"Your body has been sitting here, but you haven't. Please tell us what's up with you," Monica pleaded.

Renee sighed and placed her fork to the side of her plate. She put her napkin in her lap and twiddled with its corners as she spoke. "As I've told you all, it's just a case. Things are really bad for a little boy that I've been monitoring for a few years. It's bad for him. He's consuming my thoughts. I'm just worried about him." Renee sighed and refused to make eye contact with them. They always had a way of detecting if one another was lying or withholding information.

Kim chewed her food while she spoke. She wanted to eat as much as she could while she had the appetite to do so. "I think it's more than a case and a little boy. You have been a social worker since the day you graduated from college. You've dealt with hundreds of cases and kids over the years and they've only made you draw closer to God and pray more. You've never been this gloomy over any of them before. I'm not buying what you're trying to sell. And what is over there that you keep looking at?" Kim bucked her neck as she looked over her shoulder to see where Renee's gaze was fixed, which was on the man sitting at the booth with Kyle. Kim pepped up. "For you to be so gloomy, you sure have been giving that guy a lot of your attention tonight. Is that what has you down, you think you won't be his type?"

"Kim, what are you talking about?" Monica chimed in.

"I'm saying, he's with Kyle, so he must have money. He's not bad looking, he's actually handsome, well dressed, and well, you see her." She pointed to Renee. "Mother Theresa here with her long skirts and God-awful plaid shirts doesn't normally attract the likes of guys like them." Kim couldn't stomach anymore food so she dropped her fork on the plate and pushed it away from her.

Pam shook her head. "Kim, you can just be so rude at times. I mean, really? Renee is your sister and you're being mean to her."

Renee cleared her throat. "It's okay, Pam. What the hussy says doesn't bother me." Renee gave them a half smile to which Monica cupped her mouth to quell the laughter erupting in her. Pam's head fell back allowing her mouth to open wide as she laughed heartily as Renee continued to speak, "I'm certain I can get any man's attention I want, but the key word is 'want'. I don't want a man right now."

Kim sucked her teeth. "Whatever you two." She looked to Pam and Monica. "It's not that funny what she said." She then looked at Renee, "I am not a hussy, as I've told you all before, I'm liberated. And I guess with that comeback, you aren't so despondent after all, at least not for now." Kim, with a raised eyebrow of inquiry, stared at Renee for a minute before she took a sip of her water.

The ladies continued catching up with one another as they finished their food. They intermittently asked Renee if she was ready to open up to them about the real reason behind her gloom, but every time they asked, she responded with her disposition being about her work cases.

"Okay, ladies, well it's been fun hanging out with you all, but I have to get back to the twins and to my husband." Monica winked and laughed waiting on Kim and Renee's response. When they didn't say anything about her comment and body language, she questioned them. "What you two? No mention of me alluding to getting it on with your brother and you all being annoyed by it?" Monica clutched her chest feigning being appalled.

"Nope, I will not spend the rest of y'alls marriage battling you over telling us what you do with my brother behind closed doors. Maybe if we ignore it, you'll stop. Ain't that right, Renee?" Kim looked to Renee for her agreement, but of course, Renee's attention was somewhere else. "Here's my money for the food." Kim threw her money on the table and jumped up with her purse in her hand.

"Where are you going? Let's all walk out together," Pam said.

"I'm not leaving out of the restaurant, I just figured that I'll help my sister out and play matchmaker for the love connection she is clearly afraid to make on her own." Kim strutted away from the table slipping out of Renee's grasp as she tried to hold her back.

Pam gathered her stuff and caught up with Kim knowing she would probably need to reel her brashness in.

Monica stayed at the table settling the bill with the waiter. And Renee sat there in disbelief of Kim and her misunderstanding of Renee giving so much attention to Andrew. Kim thought she was too shy to approach him, but that wasn't necessarily true. She admitted to herself she was attracted to him in a way she hadn't experienced before. She had been telling herself the whole night that she allowed herself to stare at him for educational purposes and she never once broke the stare when he was looking at her because she was hoping, perhaps through their unspoken communication of stares, she could find out more about him. Maybe his body language would somehow tell his story. She wanted to know how to better pray for him since God hadn't lifted the burden of her doing so yet.

**

"Um, excuse me, Kyle. Sorry to bother you and your friend, but," Kim looked to Andrew, "I couldn't help but notice that during our time here, you and my sister have been staring at one another. You into her? Just too shy to say something?" Kim stood with her head slightly cocked to the side waiting for Andrew to respond. Although she was only five-three, her presence was tall and commanded attention.

Pam peeked from behind Kim to speak to the gentlemen. Nervous and embarrassed, her eyelids fluttered. "I'm sorry you all for interrupting your dinner, but my friend Kim here just doesn't know how to keep her mouth shut. Let's go, Kim." Pam tried to push Kim in the direction of the front door but Kim didn't budge.

Kyle laughed. "It's okay. Like I told you before, my wife is a very blunt woman, so I'm used to it. And Andrew here can take it, too."

"Good. Well, Andrew, would you like to get to know my sister?" Kim stared at him.

Andrew chuckled out of disbelief at Kim's bluntness. Monica and Renee finally made their way over to the table, although Renee stood back from everyone.

Kim turned around to see Renee hiding and her caramel hued fingers grabbed Renee by the arm and pulled her to her side. The motion made Renee hover Andrew. "Oh good, the other half of the subject at hand is here. Andrew, right?" She looked to Andrew for confirmation of his name, when he nodded his head in agreement, she continued on. "This is Renee. Renee, this is Andrew." Kim smiled and Kyle snickered as Renee placed her hand into Andrew's extended hand. The duo's eyes held on to each other longer than their handshake.

"See, you two are attracted to each other. So won't you just ask her for her number and we'll be on our way." Kim practically demanded Andrew.

Renee shook her head in regret of being in the restaurant with Kim at the moment. Possibly being her sister. She tried to walk away but Kim's firm grip on her elbow kept her cemented next to her.

Andrew pulled his stare away from Renee and cleared his throat. "No offense, um..." he motioned his hand in the air as if trying to recall her name.

"It's Kim. My name is Kim."

"Sorry, I guess I didn't catch it."

"I didn't throw it," Kim said sharply.

Kyle turned his head away from the gathering to try and hide his merriment of the scene unfolding in front of him.

Andrew chuckled before continuing on. "You're right, you didn't, Kim. And of course you're Renee." He said Renee's name with such tenderness that all of the women's postures relaxed. "I truly don't mean to be rude, but with what I have going on right now in my personal life, I'm not able to give a woman the attention she deserves." He looked away from Renee not wanting to see any disappointment in her eyes.

"Oh, well if you're having trouble in your life, then Renee is just the right woman for you. She's a praying woman that can pray you out of your darkness and into the marvelous light." Kim waved her hand in the air as if showcasing a ray of light.

They all heard Monica literally face palm herself in pure disbelief of Kim's words. "I'm sorry, gentlemen, for interrupting your dinner. Let's go mouth all mighty." Monica tried to usher Kim away from the table, but again she wouldn't budge.

Kim turned her head to make eye contact with each of the other ladies. "Stop acting like y'all never met me before." She looked back at Andrew whose lips were pressed tightly together trying to contain any laughter threatening to erupt out of his mouth. He cast his eyes down to prevent himself from looking at Kim's continued theatrics, and moreover, getting lost in Renee's eyes again.

"Andrew, I can tell that you and my sister are attracted to one another, so if you won't ask her for her number, then she'll just leave her business card with you. I'm certain you'll be using it." Kim waited for Renee to follow her directions, but Renee stood there with her head low willing herself to look anywhere but at Andrew. Kim knew she had to continue being bossy in order to accomplish her mission. She huffed a loud sigh. "You two, peas in a pod. Liking each other, but refusing to say it to one another." She reached into Renee's purse knowing she kept her cards in her wallet and pulled one out. She placed it on the table in front of Andrew. "Here. Have a good night you all." She smiled and walked off with her elbow locked with Renee's who was trying to distance herself from her. Kim leaned over and kissed Renee's cheek. "Although you're acting embarrassed now, I'm certain you'll thank me later on." Kim laughed and opened the door to the restaurant.

Monica and Pam stayed behind at the table. "We are so sorry for our crazy friend's antics," Monica spoke up, seeing as though Pam's shock silenced her. Monica admitted Pam had every right to be shocked at the level Kim's uncouthness reached moments earlier.

Kyle contained his laughter waiting on Andrew's response.

"That's okay. No need to apologize. Her behavior actually made me forget about my issues for the moment. Tell her I said thank you." Andrew flashed them a smile.

"Goodnight," Pam managed to say and waved at the gentleman as she headed to the door.

"Goodnight, ladies," Kyle and Andrew said one after the other as they watched Monica finally exit the restaurant.

Kyle stared at Andrew before they both erupted in laughter with their deep voices bellowing out in the restaurant. With varying stares from other patrons nearby, they simmered down remembering they were in a public place.

"Women are a trip," Kyle said as he wiped his eyes. He honestly had shed a few tears of laughter.

"Yeah, they really are."

"So are you gonna call her?" Kyle's voice presented a more serious tone.

"Naw, I don't need to bring anyone else into the mess that is my life right now." Andrew finally looked down at the card Kim had given him. *Renee Williams. Investigation Supervisor for DCFS. Hmmm, DCFS? Adoptions. She might understand my situation after all. Maybe I will call her.*

7

Renee sat on a loveseat by herself in the Sutherlands modern décor living area looking at everyone around her. She was happy that even after Pam had experienced heartbreak and inner turmoil due to her affair with a married man, she ended up finding love with Vance. He was the principal at the school where she and Kim worked at as teachers. Which brought them all to the Sutherlands home that night. Marcus Sutherland Sr., Vance's brother, knew the journey it took for Pam and Vance to finally get together.

The same time Pam was battling her demon of being with a married man, Vance was on the run from God. He felt God let his innocent father get murdered many years back. Vance ultimately gave his life back to God after denying His existence for so long and his relationship with God brought him the peace he had been missing. His conversion back to Christ helped him to finally win Pam's heart.

Marcus wanted her friends and he and his brother's friends to come together and mingle. He and his wife, Tricia, opened their home for everyone to get to know each other better. The hosts had the gut feeling that Pam and Vance would make their way to the altar soon enough and both groups of friends would interact more often than not.

Renee looked at Vance and Pam near the kitchen island chatting with Marcus and his wife. She noted Vance ogling Pam with such admiration for her. She was glad that her friend had finally found the *one* for her.

She shook her head looking over at Kim. It was obvious from Kim's flirty interaction with Darius, a good friend of both Vance and Marcus, that the two were still seeing one another. They had been introduced at Kim's school's end of the year cookout for the staff. Renee wasn't there, but Pam had filled her in on how Darius stared at Kim during the entire event and wasn't the least bit surprised when Kim put the moves on him before he had the chance to step to her.

She didn't have to look too far to her left to see her triplet brother, Keith, hugged up with Monica. She always knew those two were destined to be together after Keith accidentally knocked Monica out with a pillow at a sleepover when they were in middle school.

Everyone else was coupled up but her, and she was okay with that. There was too much going on with her emotions and prayer life to bother herself with the thoughts of being with a man. She knew the Lord would bless her with one when the time was right and she didn't think that it was the right time. Brandon was still in a coma with no signs of brain activity and her heart was still in anguish of the whereabouts of her son and his safety.

She tried not to come that night, but as usual, Kim threatened her to be in attendance. Although she wasn't scared of her sister, she knew Kim would nag and annoy her until she showed up at the Sutherland's doorstep. She avoided the drama and made her way there.

She shook her head, looking at her sister, who was visibly shorter than her, sauntering across the room towards her.

Darius stayed behind gawking at Kim. She knew she would have to add him to her prayer list. She had been praying for Kim's loose ways for years but she still hadn't changed. Maybe if she prayed for Darius and he turned over a new leaf, he would in turn help

Kim strengthen her roots and hang from a new branch. Granted she didn't know much about Darius, but if he was into Kim, then she knew he was into having sex before marriage.

Kim sat down on the couch next to her. "Sissy, I made sure you came here so that you can interact with some fun adults and take your mind off the case you say that's had you down lately." Kim gave her the side eye. "I see everyone around is enjoying themselves but you. If you would've gotten what's his name's number that night, you would be here cuddled up with him right now."

"His name is Andrew." The corners of Renee's mouth slightly curved up when she said his name.

Kim leaned into her smiling. "I caught your smile when you said his name. You must like him."

"I don't know anything about him to like him."

"That doesn't mean you can't like him. Sometimes we can just observe a person and know that they are someone we'd like and with how long you two stared at each other at dinner, you should know him well." Kim temporarily suspended her witty commentary as she observed Renee's body language. "With your slumped shoulders and sour face, I'm really starting to think not having a man is the real reason you've been so out of touch with us lately. Monica's married. Pam has Vance now, and you know I'm content with or without one as long as my needs get satisfied, if you know what I mean." Kim winked. "Are you sad, sissy, that you're alone? Are you feeling like God has forgotten about you?" It seemed as if Kim loved hearing herself speak. She didn't even allow Renee to attempt to answer any of her questions before she continued on, "If you would just loosen up a bit, let your hair down some, you could attract a man to spend time with. Has he called you yet?"

"No." Renee almost sounded disappointed.

"You can't always wait on them to make the first move. Sometimes you have to."

"Whatever, Kim."

"I'm serious. See he may be your type after all. He's not forward either. You probably couldn't handle the type of guys I date." Kim looked up and caught Darius staring at her. She smirked at him.

"Kim." Renee sighed. "Life is not just about men for women. How many times have I told you that God has called me to pray and intercede for others? I'm fine with that. You need to learn to be fine with the way I am."

"But I just want you to have fun, enjoy your life more. We're still so young. Enjoy yourself." Kim shook Renee's shoulders hoping to shake her into a more carefree and jovial person.

"You have your definition of fun, and I have mine." Renee patted Kim's knee as she stood up from the couch to get away from her sister. She was hoping to go to the bathroom and come out of it with a brilliant reason for why she needed to excuse herself from the party. She just wanted to go home and be alone, or at least be alone with her worship music and her prayers.

She made her way past Monica and Keith and stopped dead in her tracks when she overheard Marcus whispering to Vance that he had just gotten a promotion within the bureau. *FBI? He's an agent? Interesting.*

She decided she wouldn't leave so soon after all. She wanted to stay and learn more about Vance's brother, Marcus.

8

Andrew sat in the dark in his condo with a piercing headache. He was never the type to take medicine for pain, he would suffer through it until it subsided. Besides, he knew the root of his headache—stressing over what to do about his father, Charles. He knew as long as he didn't resolve the issue, the looming headache would always interrupt him from having a seemingly peaceful evening.

He smirked, thinking that at least he had returned to some type of normalcy with his clients. The NBA season was soon to start and he had been busying himself with securing his clients contracts with teams and endorsement deals. He was grateful that not only did he still have Kyle as a client, even though Kyle's basketball career was over, but that he had added more clients to his roster. The amount of clients he had and the work he had to do for each of them kept him busy and made it easier for him to ignore the constant phone calls from his family and at times, help him to temporarily ignore the hatred and confusion he felt for his father.

He wasn't much of a drinker but he looked at the long neck beer bottle in his hand and then down at his beer gut forming. He laughed as he got up from his couch and made his way to the kitchen. He discarded the remains of the beer in his hand in the trash and headed to the refrigerator. He opened it up and snatched the two six packs of beer he had in there and dumped them in the garbage as well. He went back to his living area and lowered himself to the floor.

Two-hundred pushups and three-hundred sit-ups later, he laid on the floor sweaty and battling the rage he was carrying for his father that he just couldn't shake. *How could he rape Marie?* That question kept haunting his inner thoughts.

He rolled over on his back and slightly lifted his head to stare at his stomach. He laughed at himself thinking that the quick workout he pressed through would rid his stomach of the beers he had been consuming for weeks. However, he nodded his head in approval still seeing the remnants of his six pack. He let his head drop back to the floor and the tenor in his voice took up space in his home as he chuckled at himself. "I am pitiful. I'm here alone wallowing in someone else's mistake."

He gathered himself from the floor and collapsed again on his couch. It was still dark in the room but he could see the white business card resting on the ottoman he propped his feet on. He leaned forward and grabbed it and smiled thinking about who it belonged to. She was beautiful. He now knew her name and had been repeating it to himself at any given time of the day since he last saw her at the restaurant. He thought it fit her so well.

Am I really attracted to her, or is it the fact that she's a social worker and may know how I feel as an adopted child the reason why I can't stop thinking about her? Andrew dismissed the thoughts in his head and threw the card away from him. It didn't land too far away from him though. His phone rang, but he didn't answer it. It was his personal cell phone, not the one he used for his clients to handle business so he knew it wasn't anyone other than his adoptive mom, dad, or brother and sister. He still wasn't ready to speak to any of them.

Melanie and Marie had agreed to give him some space before they left the island, so he knew it wasn't them. Besides, he had texted Melanie earlier that day to tell her that he was alright and to give Marie a hug for him.

He rubbed his face again and let his head fall to the side. He stared at the card staring back at him on the couch with Renee's name, work number, and cell number on it. "What the hell." He reached for his personal cell phone and dialed her number. The phone rang. He pulled the phone away from his face to check the time. It was only 8:30 p.m. He reasoned it wasn't too late to call her and continued to let it ring. *Maybe she's with her man and can't answer.* He pulled the phone away from his face preparing to end the call when he heard what he thought was the sweetest most angelic voice say hello into the phone. He quickly put the phone back up to his ear. "Hello." He played with the drawstring on his jogging pants.

"Hello. Who is this?"

"Uh, this is Andrew." He couldn't understand why he felt like a young school boy holding his breath waiting for his crush to check yes or no if she liked him on the note he passed her in class.

"Andrew?" Renee said his name as if questioning where and how she met him although she knew very well who he was. She had been thinking about him nonstop since the first time she laid eyes on him. She inwardly laughed at herself. Something she hadn't done all day.

Andrew sat up on the couch. "Uh, yeah, Andrew. I saw you on the island for Karen and Kyle's wedding, and then I saw you at the restaurant. Remember? Your sister gave me your card instead of you giving it to me."

Renee didn't respond yet.

Maybe she really doesn't know who I am. "I guess I wasn't too easy on the eyes, hunh?" Andrew furrowed his eyebrows at what he said. It slipped out, but he guess he said it in an attempt to gauge her interest in him.

If only you knew how handsome you are to me, Renee thought inwardly. She got up from kneeling on the floor. She had been interceding for Brandon, her son, and her current caller, Andrew. She was glad that she had said her last amen and had caught him before he hung up the phone. She knew it had been ringing longer than most people would allow a phone to ring nowadays, but praying was her focus. She paused before speaking, hoping to remove any of the excitement that was brewing in her after hearing his voice. "Yes, I remember you now. How are you doing?"

The sincerity and sweetness in her voice made him want to tell her everything that had been going on with him, but he decided against it. "I'm okay."

"You don't sound like everything's okay." In spite of them not knowing each other, Renee wished he would open up to her. She felt if he told her what

93

had him sounding in despair, it would help her target her prayers and uproot it from his life. She wouldn't push him though. She didn't even know him.

"Yeah, I have some things going on in my personal life. That's kind of why I called you."

Her heart sank wondering if he was having trouble with his woman. *But why call me if that's the case?* In that moment, she recognized her attraction to him was more than a call to pray for him, but with what she had going on in her life, she knew she couldn't afford nor had the desire to entertain a man.

He had been silent for a minute causing her curiosity to get the best of her. "Andrew, why did you call me?" She became more vocal than she normally would with a man.

"Um, I see that you're a social worker, you work for DCFS and I was just wondering if maybe I talked to you about my situation. It might help me be able to make some kind of sense of it, possibly let go of some of this rage I've been carrying." *I didn't mean to say rage to her, although that's what I've been feeling. I don't want to scare her off.*

She was silent on the other end of the phone. He bit the inside of his lip waiting on her to respond.

He needs my help with getting his kids back? What did he do to lose them? She went into advocate mode for his children. She stopped pacing the floor and cleared her throat. "Andrew, if you were negligent with their well-being, harmed them, and the state took them, it may be a long road to get them back, if ever." Her forehead creased as she became distraught imagining all the bad things he could've done to get his children taken away from him. Which made her blurt out her next question. "And where was there mother in all of this?"

Andrew sat up on the couch. "Renee, them? I don't have any kids if that's what you're thinking."

"Oh." Renee finally stopped pacing the floor. She walked from her bedroom to her living room and sat on her couch. "I'm sorry for jumping to conclusions and assuming-"

"No, I'm sorry for not being straight forward with you from the moment you picked up the phone."

They both chuckled, now more at ease with one another.

He was still hung up on the tenderness in her voice, and to add to that the way she was quick to come to children's defense. Her compassion for kids moved him in ways he hadn't been moved by a woman in a long time, if ever. "So let me just come out and say it. My birth mother gave me up for adoption when I was four."

"Okay." Renee relaxed on the couch. *Well at least he doesn't have kids if we decided to get together. Wait. No. This man hasn't said he likes me like that. I can't jump the gun, nor should I.* "I can understand how you might feel like you can talk to me about being adopted since I'm a social worker. So did you just find out recently that you were adopted?"

"No, I've known all of my life."

"So if you've known about it all of this time, why are you so enraged now, or have you been that way all of your life?"

Andrew breathed a deep sigh of frustration. "No, I had no reason to be upset before recently. Although I've wanted to know my birth parents and family my whole life, I still loved and had so much respect for my adoptive parents. They were great to me."

"So why the rage?"

Andrew was silent.

"It's okay if you don't want to talk about it. Just know that I've been praying for you. I know God will work things out for you in time."

Andrew could feel his pulse in his throat and he barely blinked. He had never met a woman who prayed for him. This beautiful woman with the sweetest voice he'd ever heard was praying for him without even knowing him or what was going on in his life. His posture relaxed and he felt so much comfortable just being on the phone with her.

"Drew?" Renee's face scrunched up wondering if he was even still on the phone.

She called me Drew. I loved the way she said it. No. You didn't call her to flirt or fantasize about being with her. He cleared his throat. "Yes?"

"What is it then? Whatever you tell me is safe with me."

I bet it is. He smiled. She was the only one that had been making him do that lately. "Renee, I was recently reconnected with my mother."

"Oh goody." Renee smiled at the news, but then took on a more serious tone. "If everything has been good, why the rage, if you don't mind me asking?"

He huffed. "Well, she was raped and conceived me, that's why she gave me up for adoption."

"I'm sorry to hear that." Things were starting to make sense to her. *Maybe his relationship is strained with his birth mother. Maybe he feels some type of way after finding out he was the product of rape.* "Just give it some time with her. I'm sure she'll come around soon enough. And you know, you can't blame yourself for how you got here."

He thought it was cute how she thought she had his dilemma figured out. Her trying to console him added to the list of reasons to like her. He would have given anything to sit next to her and stare into her eyes as he bore his soul to her. "Renee, my relationship with my birth mother is going great, and I don't blame myself because I'm the product of a rape. I'm just still in disbelief about it all and I don't know what to do next." His shoulders slumped and he let out a long sigh as he rubbed the fluffy waves on his head. He realized he needed to get his hair cut again first thing in the morning.

"So is he in jail for what he did? Do you want to confront him?" Renee now sat Indian style on her couch twiddling with the hem of her long nightgown. She loved the deep sound of his voice, she just wished it wasn't filled with so much anguish. She was enjoying talking to him, but she preferred a different subject matter. Spending much of her day dealing with mistreated kids, not to mention the turmoil she was experiencing over knowing nothing about her son she gave up, she just wanted a reprieve from it all. *Maybe God is pushing me until I do something about it?*

"I want to confront him, I just don't know if I'll be able to control myself when and if I do."

"So you know who he is?"

"Yes." Andrew shook his head as he rubbed his forehead.

"Okay, so what's stopping you then?"

"Maybe we should talk about this over dinner."

9

Renee sat in the popular coffee shop in the Edgewater area of Chicago waiting for Andrew to arrive. He offered to pick her up, but not wanting it to feel like a date, she simply agreed to meet him there.

She smiled a little as she looked down at her outfit thinking about how her coworkers teased her earlier that day at work. They all agreed that she must had special plans that evening because of what she wore to work. As opposed to her usual ankle length skirts and plaid button up, she opted to put on a black A-line skirt that hit just at her knee and a tan chiffon blouse with black polka dots. It had puffy sleeves and a scarf attached to the mock neck. She elected to tie the scarf in a cute bow. Amina was shocked to see that she actually had a girlish figure. No one at work knew she had an hourglass figure under the shapeless clothes she wore to work daily. If it weren't for Kim, she wouldn't even have had the outfit as an option, but with Kim being tired of how she dressed, she intermittently put clothes in Renee's closet.

Renee had never seen the outfit before that morning, but when she woke up, the realization of meeting Andrew for coffee after work hit her and she wanted to wear something other than her ordinary style. She would never wear something risqué such as showing her ample cleavage or pants so tight that one could see what size underwear she wore. Sadly, Ted had beaten the thought of her dressing more trendy and hip out of her. She wasn't always like the way she had become to be. Granted she always had her ear to the Lord, but she was once more relaxed an open to things, thus how she ended up with Ted back in undergrad. She met him in the cafeteria one day. She was sitting alone, reviewing her notes when he came and made himself comfortable at her table. He seemed harmless, so she talked to him for a while before she had to leave to take a test. He asked her out before she left but she told him if he wanted to see her again then he would meet her at the campus bible study that night at the student center.

Ted showed up at the next bible study, and unbeknownst to her, pretended to be so into God and a scholar of the bible. He courted her the way she wanted him to for six months before he started pressuring her to have sex. She knew it wasn't right, seeing as though she studied the bible all of the time, but she ignored the voice of God not to go down that path with Ted and slept with him. Her heart was already his by that time. The longer they were together, the more controlling he became of her— picking out what she could wear, where she could go, and even closing her off from the sisterhood for a while.

She brought herself back from memory lane after hearing the chime on the door signaling that someone had either entered or exited the shop. She looked to see Andrew coming towards her. His full lips called her even though he said nothing.

His skin was chocolaty rich and looked so creamy to her. He looked as if he could be the spokesperson for Dove's male body wash line if they had one. She took a deep breath, trying to even her breathing. He was even more handsome that she remembered him to be. *Be calm, this is not a date. He's already said he just wants to talk to me because of my profession. So why did I get all cute for him then? Especially put this lipstick on. I bet it doesn't even fit me.* She puckered her lips trying to even out the color but then grabbed a napkin on the table ready to wipe it completely off.

Andrew made it to the table just as she had the napkin up to her lips. He paused trying to settle the nerves fraying his thoughts. He only reached out to her because he thought talking to her based on what she did would somehow help him figure out what to do with Charles, but standing in front of her, staring at her with the deep matte burgundy lipstick on her supple lips made him lose his concentration. His mind quickly flashed back to the first time he saw her. How beautiful she was as the soft breeze on the island lightly lifted her dark brown hair off of her shoulders and outlined her delicate neck.

"Drew? Drew? How are you?"

"Hunh?" He shook his head trying to regain focus of the moment.

She stood up in front of him. "You were just standing there staring at me. I asked how you're doing today."

He laughed as he tucked her seat in under her before he took his seat. "I'm sorry, I just got lost in thought for a second. I've been doing that a lot lately."

"Yeah, me, too." Renee frowned.

Andrew noted her slumped shoulders and the sadness that had crept into her eyes. "We came here to talk about me, but is everything okay with you?"

She waved him off. "Yeah, everything's fine with me. I just have some cases, some kids that I've been thinking a lot about lately."

"I bet. If you don't feel like listening to my story, I can understand. We can talk about anything you like or nothing at all. If you're ready to go, we can leave, too."

"Oh no, I'm fine. This is my calling to help others in need, especially when it comes to adoptions and whatnot."

The corners of Andrew's mouth tilted up, grateful that she wasn't ready to leave him yet. "But yeah, you have to take care of yourself, too. If the cases are weighing you down too much, then maybe you need to take a break from them. Take a vacation."

Despite her nervousness being around him, Renee focused to keep direct eye contact with him. Something she was soon regretting, because with the way he was staring at her, she didn't know if her emotions, her body, her senses could take being under his deep, penetrating stare any longer. "If it isn't the pot calling the kettle black." She laughed a little, but his intense stare never wavered from her.

"Hunh?"

"You're telling me I need to take a step back from what I'm dealing with if it's making me sad, but excuse me for being blunt, something which I rarely ever do, but when I first saw you on the island, with as handsome as you are…" *Did I really just say that out loud? I guess I did since that slow smile is creeping across his face. Okay, no more slipups. You're here to do the work of the Lord and that's it.* "…you were looking quite, how should I say it…" Her eyes shifted from side to side searching for the right words to say that wouldn't offend him.

He laughed. "Just say it."

"I'm sorry, but you were looking rough when I first saw you. Handsome but rough." *No, you said it again.* Renee broke eye contact with him and looked anywhere around the coffee shop but at him. Although she didn't know the song that was playing, she heard the soulful songstress's words clearly "…he possesses an enchantment…"

"Renee, it's okay. You don't have to be embarrassed that you've called me handsome twice within the last few minutes." He struggled to suppress the laughter brewing in him.

Small beads of perspiration formed on her forehead and she hadn't made eye contact with him again since the end of her statement. He could tell she was nervous and embarrassed as she loosened the bow around her neck. "Really, it's okay. I think that you are absolutely beautiful. I mean beautiful." He sat, leaning into the table with his hands interlaced waiting for her to look at him or at least respond to him.

She slowly turned her head back towards him.

He locked eyes with her again before speaking. "And you're right, it's crazy how we can always give advice to others about their situation and encourage them but can hardly ever seem to take our own advice or encourage ourselves. I just think my situation is personal versus your occupation being something that you can step away from daily."

With a snip in her tone, she spoke, "That's the thing, when you're called to do something, you *can't* just walk away from it whenever the going gets tough, no matter how much you may want to." He retreated in his seat and she quickly regretted how harsh she must've sounded talking to him. She extended her hand to him. "I'm sorry, I wasn't trying to be callous. I'm just passionate about what I do, so whenever the subject comes up, I defend my calling if need be."

"No worries. Doing what you do, I wouldn't have it any other way for you but to be as passionate as you are. Do you want to order something now?"

"Sure." She told him what she wanted and breathed a deep sigh of relief as he left the table to place their orders.

She needed a moment to recompose herself. The night was not going as it should be for her. She had come there dressed out of character, experienced shortness of breath whenever he looked at her too long, admitted to him that he was handsome, and probably made him think she had an attitude problem when she had to get snippy with him. Yeah, the night wasn't what she had in mind up to the point.

He soon returned to the table with her Caesar chicken salad and a Carmel Macchiato. His order mirrored hers.

He smiled when he placed both their trays on the table. "I wasn't copying you with my food choices, this is just honestly one of my favorite things to eat."

"No problem. It's my favorite whenever I do eat out."

"Okay, cool." Andrew picked up his fork ready to chow down, but Renee called his name, "Andrew, how about we pray together?"

With the tenderness her eyes held and the cute apprehension he heard in her voice, he would've easily said yes to any request she made of him. He cleared his throat hoping it would free his mind of the ever growing attraction he was gaining for the beautiful woman with the long, dark brown, wavy hair in front of him. However, that was a dilemma for him, he knew he was in no state of mind to entertain a woman. "Sure."

"Okay, bow your head," Renee said.

He closed his eyes and lowered his head again. He jumped a little when he felt her soft hands grip his on the table. *Man, her hands are really soft,* Andrew thought.

"Lord God, we thank You for this food. We ask that You would purify it and bless the hands that prepared it. We thank You God for blessing this fellowship between Andrew and me." She squeezed one of his hands even tighter.

He loosened up some.

"We thank You, God, that we would glean from one another what You would have us to and that we would hear from You always and obey Your commands..." Renee let her words trail off as she felt herself getting ready to pray in an unknown language. Although she ignored the sisterhood whenever they teased her about being so deep in God, she didn't quite know Andrew yet and where his relationship with God was. She was learning not to throw her religion or rather her relationship with God up in everyone's face, everyone except for the sisterhood. She didn't want to scare him by speaking in tongues, so she paused. She felt his firm grip on her hand as she slightly lifted her head and opened one eye to look at him. He seemed more relaxed than before she had started praying, but she still thought it was best to end the prayer. "In Jesus' name, Amen."

"Amen." Andrew smiled as he reluctantly loosed his grip on her hand.

"So, what's up?" She stared at him as she ate some of her salad. She immediately covered her mouth with her napkin as she chewed.

His lips quickly curved up into a smile. "It's okay. You don't have to sit here the entire time with me covering your mouth while you chew." He began to chew.

She dabbed at the corners of her mouth with her napkin before placing it on the table. She smiled.

"Well, I just figured since you've probably placed a lot of kids and helped with their adoptions then maybe you could share some stories with me. Whether they be good or bad." His jaws tightened and his body tensed at the end of his statement.

Renee instinctively grabbed his hand and caressed it trying to comfort him. They locked eyes and shared that same kismet kind of moment they had when they crossed each other's paths in the hallway during Kyle and Karen's wedding reception. She slowly pulled her hand back from covering his as she noted the pained expression leave his face. His mouth and body fully relaxed again.

"Are you sure you want me to tell you about the bad adoption stories?" Her eyebrows crumpled, searching his eyes for the truth.

He rubbed his face in frustration before he sat back in his chair. "Yes. Maybe there will be something you'll share with me to help me better figure out my situation."

"Okay." She put her fork down. "Well..." She shared as many memorable good endings as she could with him but he egged her on to tell of the not so happy ones as well. By her fourth tragic adoption story, he was visibly tense, grinding his teeth. "Andrew, you said me sharing stories with you might help you, but the light seems to be getting darker and darker around you."

He sighed. "I feel like I'm in a dark tunnel. I see the exits on both sides, I just don't know what I'll find on the other side of either opening." He lowered his head into his hands and kept it there.

Renee was quiet. She did the only thing she knew how to do in times like these, she grabbed his hands to pray. He looked up at her but kept his arms stiff, preventing her from pulling his hands closer to her. The longer he looked into her mesmerizing eyes to help him, the more he relaxed his muscles until his arms were outstretched across the table. Although the coffee shop was bustling with patrons, Renee didn't care who heard her prayer. She saw that Andrew was in distress and she knew she had the remedy to aide him. It was as if prayer had become her penance for abandoning her son. "Bow your head with me." She closed her eyes and lowered her head. "Lord God, we thank You that You are Jehovah Shalom, the God of Peace, so we call on you to do just that, be the God of peace in our lives. We need you God, I know I need you." A tear seeped from her eye.

Andrew thought he heard suffering in her voice and looked up at her. He didn't know if she was moved by her prayer or if it was that unknown turmoil he saw in her eyes at times when he looked at her. She was so beautiful to him. The way her hair draped as her head hung low. He couldn't see much of her face, but his lips formed a weak smile noting just how naturally beautiful she was. Her cocoa skin was blemish free and looked so soft. He knew it had to be since her hands were so soft. She didn't know much about him, only the little he told her about his adoption and here she was getting choked up and praying for him, like no one ever had—like she really cared about him. Everything about her moved him. He tuned back just when she seemed to be ending the prayer.

"And God, we thank You that it's already done. Give Andrew the answers he needs surrounding his situation, Lord. Grant him peace. Lord, please grant me peace."

Andrew squeezed her hands as he watched the steady stream of tears fall from her face and puddle on the table. "In Jesus' name we pray. Amen," Renee spoke but kept her head low as she cleared her throat.

He kept a firm hold on one of her hands and released the other to grab a napkin. He held the napkin near her face and began to dab at her tears as she slowly lifted her head. He stared into her red eyes wishing that he could fight whatever battle for her that she seemed to be losing.

"Thank you." She was barely audible as she took the napkin from him and fully dried her face.

He never let go of her other hand. He cleared his throat. "No, thank you. I feel better than what I did before I came here. You seem to have that effect on me."

She gave him a half smile as she sniffled.

"No seriously. I know I didn't tell you anymore about my adoption than I did on the phone, but you still managed to comfort me. I just wish I could do the same for you."

Renee tried to pull her hand from his. Too many emotions were bubbling up inside of her. He wouldn't release her hand and she submitted to herself that that was okay too, because little did he know, his presence was somehow encouraging her with what to do next. She used her free hand to grab her cup and sip some water before she spoke to him again. She knew she sounded like a frog rebuilding her facade. "What do you mean comfort me? I'm fine."

He leaned in closer to the table and managed to pry her other hand from under her chin. He caressed the back of both of her hands as he looked into her eyes. "I admit I've worn my worry for a while. When most people ask if I'm okay they settle for my fake smile and dismissal of their concern, but you don't. I don't know how you do it, but you see pain in me that I don't even mention. When you look into my eyes, you make me forget my problems and make me try to figure out how to help you with the anguish I see in you."

This time she pulled her hands away from him firm enough causing him to finally release them. She placed them on her lap and sat up straight. "I'll tell you just like I tell anyone else who asks, I'm fine. It's just the stress of some of these cases that have me burned lately. Other than that, I'm fine." She tried to sit up erect for as long as she could under his stare, but the longer he looked at her, the sooner she slumped into her seat until he could only see the top of her head and her chin resting on her chest. His shoulders shook noticeably and he chuckled before he spoke. Not because there was anything funny at the moment, but because everything about her was cute and intriguing to him. A chuckle was all he could come up with. "Renee?"

She didn't answer him.

"Renee?"

Knowing it was rude to continue ignoring him, she finally looked up at him.

He smiled. "I know we're still getting to know each other, so I understand if you're not ready to share some things with me just yet, but I hope we can continue this friendship..."

Friends? Well, God, you heard what he said. We'll just be friends. So would you tell my emotions and hormones that so they can stop overreacting whenever I think of him or see him? She tuned back in to what he was saying.

"...right about now, I need you in my life."

She took a deep breath. "Friends. I'm okay with us just being friends."

His eyebrows creased as he listened to how she overemphasized the word "friends". He knew he could never only just be her friend, but until he figured out what he was going to do concerning his dad, he didn't want to get involved with her romantically, just yet.

She gathered her purse and stood up.

He followed suit. "You ready to go?"

"Yes." She barely made eye contact with him.

113

"Okay. I'll walk you to your car."

"Thanks." She walked ahead of him and led him to her car. "Thanks again." She never faced him again as she lowered herself into her seat.

He could see the tension in her stiff body and the fact that she never made eye contact with him again worried him. He bent down to look into the car. "Thank you for tonight, I know I didn't talk much but your prayer and presence really did comfort me."

"Just doing the Lord's work." She started the car never looking over at him.

"Renee?"

She hated the way he said her name. The warmness in his voice was contrary to him saying they were just friends earlier. Her insides were all jumbled up over him. "Yes?"

"Will you look at me please?"

She slowly looked at him, into his eyes. His dark brown eyes searched hers for answers to why her behavior shifted with him. He wished he could stare into them all night, but he had to let her go. He wanted to be respectful of her time and he knew it was time to check in with Marie and Melanie again to let them know that he was okay. "Will you please call me and let me know that you made it home alright?"

"Sure."

He stepped back and closed her door.

She sped off, intermittently looking back at him in her rearview mirror. She didn't know what would become of the evening when it first started. Ending it, she was more confused about how attracted she was to Andrew versus being unsure of his interest in her. She felt she did gain one thing from him, seeing his unrest at his age over his adoption let her know she didn't want that fate for her son. Andrew helped her to see that she had to find her son as soon as possible. No matter what it was going to take.

10

Kim had grown tired of Renee ignoring her calls or not coming over to the Sunday dinners their parents hosted. She knew she hadn't even stopped by to see the twins, and that was unusual seeing as though none of them ever went a week without getting their quality time in with the adorable babies. She had a spare key to Renee's apartment and she was ready to use it.

It was a Tuesday evening. She knew Renee was off work, there was nothing going on at her church, and plus she saw her sister's car parked outside of the apartment building. She stood right outside of Renee's apartment door and knocked on it. No answer. She put her ear up to the door and strained to hear the movement on the other side. She banged on the door. Still no answer.

If Renee thought not answering the door would send Kim packing, then she really didn't know her. "I gave you the chance to let me in on your own." Kim's voice bellowed in the hallway as she inserted her key into one of the doors lock chambers. She twisted the doorknob but it still didn't open. She needed to unlock the other lock. She inserted the key into it and twisted it until it unlocked. She then twisted the knob and pushed the door open, but it only gave her a sliver of insight into Renee's homely apartment. Renee had the link chain in place across the door. She stuck her foot in the opening of the door and then stuck as much of her head into the tight space as she could. Her big doe eyes scanned the bit of the apartment that she could see from her limited viewpoint. "Renee," she screamed out. "I know you're in here. Undo this chain right now."

"No," Renee said from her kitchen out of Kim's vantage point. She had been crying since she'd been home. She didn't want Kim to see her red eyes and hear her stuffy voice. Kim would know for certain that something was wrong with her.

"Renee, open this door right now. Don't act like you don't know me. I'll get it open your way or my way." Kim leaned even more of her petite weight against the door.

117

"Kim. I know why you're here. I promise I'm alright. I've just been swamped with my caseloads. I promise I'll hang out with you all soon. Go home. I'll call you later."

"Yeah, okay." Kim didn't know which part of her short body was the safest to use, but she knew it was the only way she'd be able to force her way into the apartment. She looked down at her feet and was glad that for once she had left her house in gym shoes rather than her normal four inch heels she wore daily. She turned her back to the door and braced her right foot flat against it. She leaned her upper body forward and lifted her bent right leg away from the door. She channeled all of her energy into her leg as her foot made contact with the door as hard as it could. She allowed her leg to extend out behind her until she heard the chain rip from its bracket on the door. The door flew open.

"Kim!" Renee screamed as she watched Kim plow through her door as if she were a superhero. "Why did you do that? I told you I would call you." Renee folded her arms tightly across her chest as she stared incredulously at her sister.

Kim stared at Renee unashamed as she walked towards her with her hands on her hips. She came within an arm's length of Renee and scanned her from head to toe.

At that point, Renee wasn't sure what Kim would do to her. They were raised to love and respect one another. They never got into physical altercations growing up and only did minor bickering here and there in regards to their varying viewpoints on life. Renee knew Kim could be unpredictable and erratic at times, but as frustrated as she appeared, she hoped Kim wasn't crazy enough to try and physically harm her.

Kim's slender nostrils flared as she stood flat footed with one foot out in front of the other. She tapped her forward foot slowly on the floor as her hands were pasted on her hips. She ran her tongue across her teeth and zoomed in her stare on Renee.

"Would you just say something already?" Renee stared back at Kim, but not as strong as Kim's intense stare.

Kim rotated her head and surveyed her surroundings before putting her attention back on Renee.

Renee was getting annoyed with Kim's silence. "You can start off by apologizing for busting through my door like that and tell me when you plan to give me the money to fix it." Renee brushed past Kim and walked to the door to assess its damage. She closed and locked it after not seeing any real harm having been done to it.

Kim stared heatedly at Renee. She finally decided to speak via a clipped tone. "You're crazy if you think I'm concerned about your door more than I am about you."

"I told you I was alright."

"The same way you told us you were alright when Ted had you cooped up for days at a time because he had beaten you so badly and didn't want us to know what he was doing to you. Neither of you did." Tears spilled from Kim's big yes.

Renee hugged Kim. "Aww, sissy. I'm sorry I haven't been calling and seeing you like you want me to, but I told you I'm okay. Just busy."

Kim wiped her face of her remaining tears as she pushed Renee back from her. "You know what, I'm sick of you. We're sisters, we're two of triplets. We share a bond closer than most siblings do and yet you don't come to me when you're going through major stuff. You didn't tell me what was going on in undergrad with you and Ted and it seems like you're keeping something major from me now. Only this time I don't see any signs that someone has been abusing you." Kim narrowed her round eyes in on Renee. "It's warm outside. There's no need for that long sleeve shirt or that awful long skirt of yours, unless...don't tell me that you've gotten with Andrew and he's beating on you already. I'll kill him." Kim lunged forward at Renee and began tugging on her clothes trying to see her skin underneath.

Renee slapped at Kim's hand as she backed away from her. "Stop it, crazy woman. Stop it." Renee raised her voice loud and high with her last words. "I will never be another man's punching bag."

Kim acquiesced and backed up some from Renee. She had worked herself into a frenzy and she was hot. Renee never ran her air conditioner, even when it was hot as it was at the end of the summer. "I'll be crazy over you if I need to be." She went into Renee's kitchen, grabbed a glass from the cabinet, and poured herself some water from the refrigerator.

Renee shook her head staring at Kim's every move. "You really are something else."

"I sure am." Kim smacked her lips. "You never tell me anything. I only found out about you getting an abortion because Monica was frustrated with you. She berated and reminded you that y'all had did the same thing in the past so you needed to stop being so judgmental of her. And again, I only knew about what Ted was doing to you because I investigated and butted my nose in where you didn't want it to be." Kim folded her arms across her chest and deliberately raised an eyebrow at Renee.

❦

"Sissy. Thank you for caring about me so much. I love you, too." Renee, smiling, walked over to Kim and wrapped her arms around her.

Kim didn't return the embrace. "Yeah, yeah, whatever." She wiggled her way out of Renee's arms. "Enough with the mushy stuff, I'm hungry. What do you have to eat?"

Thank God, Renee thought and shook her head as she watched her sister rummage through her cabinets and refrigerator looking for food. She was grateful that Kim's presence was momentarily relieving her from thoughts of her son.

11

Andrew sat in his car wondering how he wasn't even looking to meet a woman let alone a woman like Renee at that point in his life, yet she was quickly winning him over. He bet she didn't even know the affect she was having on him. He rubbed his face in wonder and racked his brain trying to figure out her many different moods. One minute she was confident as she prayed and the next minute she seemed so overcome with emotions that she could only express herself with tears. And then in the next moment she was so compassionate as she held his hand trying to encourage and support him even though he hadn't fully disclosed everything about his adoption. She didn't seem to care about the details. She was more concerned about how it was affecting him, but then she became withdrawn and barely made eye contact with him the rest of the evening. *Did I do something to make her withdraw from me? What is gnawing at her?* Although he would much rather ignore his father forever, he knew he needed to address his personal issues before stepping to Renee, but there was something about her that made him want to be there for her and comfort her, too.

He started his car and Nas's *Illmatic* album filled it. He was ready to bob his head and get lost in the lyrics of his favorite track playing but his phone vibrated. It was his personal cell phone. He wasn't tempted to answer it, but remembering Renee asking God to give him peace through what He was going through, he wondered if responding to whoever was trying to contact him might offer him some relief. He pulled his phone from its holster on his waist and breathed a sigh of relief as he saw Melanie's name headlining the text: *I can only imagine how you're still feeling, but please call me back or text me. You know Mom is really worried about you and I kind of am too, brother! Lol.*

He smiled at her calling him brother. He knew they had many more memories to build before they had that sister brother bond he had with his other sister, but he was grateful that she wasn't being as closed off with him as she was in the beginning after

ANITA DAVIS

the discovery that they indeed were brother and sister.

He scrolled through a few more unread texts to see that many were from his adoptive family, he dismissed them all. He laughed out loud at the texts Marie sent him. There were no spaces in between the words but he understood what she had said and her worry of him. He decided to text Melanie back: *Hey. Thanks for checking up on me. I'm cool. Meet me over at Mom's?* He pressed send. But immediately texted her again: *Think we should call her before we show up? You never know what we might see now that your mom and dad are back together. Lol.*

She texted back in no time: *Lol. Don't worry. I'm over here now. She's fully dressed and so is my dad.*

He texted her back: *Lol. Ok.*

***

"Hey, Drew." Marie stood in the doorway with her arms outstretched waiting for Andrew to make his way to her. She had heard him pull up into the driveway and the anticipation of seeing his face again since the island forced her to stand in the doorway ready to greet him before he even exited his car.

"Hi, Mom." He smiled as she enveloped him in her embrace. If it weren't for the unknown man sitting

125

next to Melanie on the couch he might have taken that moment to breakdown in her arms. There was still so much confusion and pinned up anger inside of him that Marie's warm and inviting embrace beckoned a cry out of him, but he wouldn't breakdown in front of a complete stranger. He cleared his throat, dismissing his emotions that had formed there.

"Come in. Oh I've missed you so much." She looped her arm with his and pinched his cheeks as they made their way over to the others in the living room.

Andrew helped her to an arm chair and walked over to shake Melanie's father's hand.

"Mr. Daniels. Good evening, sir."

"Hey, Drew. You can call me Harold." Harold smiled and nodded his head as he gripped Andrew's hand.

"Okay, Harold." Andrew turned to Melanie. She stared back at him trying to contain her laughter.

Marie saw the curious look on Andrew's face and the smile on Melanie's. She wished Melanie wouldn't do Andrew the way she did him sometimes. "Oh stop being silly and introduce your brother to your boyfriend." Marie stared at Melanie.

Melanie shot her mother an incredulous look.

"What, because I called him your boyfriend?" She smiled at Aaron as his pale complexion turned red. Being white, he couldn't hide it when he was embarrassed or blushing.

"Ma." Melanie chided her mother.

"I can't help myself. He's the first man you've ever brought home to me."

Melanie raised her hand and her mouth flew open but Marie quickly stifled her protest. "We can't count that guy from way back when. I wasn't in my right mind then." A quietness fell in the room. Aaron was the only one that wasn't privy to how Marie used to be. She was so lively now, but only a year ago and years before, she was so depressed from being raped and then giving up her son, Andrew, when he was four. But since she had reconnected with him and remarried Harold, Melanie's father, she was determined to make the rest of her years, the best of her years. "He's cute. He's nice. Introduce him to your brother so I can chat with my son." Marie sat, smiling.

Melanie shook her head in awe of Marie's new demeanor and attitude. She wish she had the new Marie for a mother growing up, but she would settle for enjoying her now and for the rest of their lives. Melanie kept her hand interlaced with Aaron's as they sat on the couch next to one another. She looked up at Andrew standing near her end of the couch. "Drew, this is Aaron, my boyfriend." Saying his name and title made her smile like a school girl in love for the first time. "And Aaron, this is my brother, Drew."

Again, Andrew waited to see if Melanie would shiver with disgust as she often had before whenever she had to refer to him as her brother, he remembered she hadn't done it the last few times he was around her either. He smiled inwardly knowing they really were making progress. "Nice to meet you, Aaron." He extended his arm out and Aaron stood and shook his hand firmly.

"Nice to meet you, too." Aaron said in his cool tone.

"Well, now that the introductions are out of the way, Harold, why don't you take Aaron in the basement and show him your coin collection?"

"Ma, really?" Melanie's eyebrows crumpled as she stared at Marie. "Aaron can understand if we want to speak to Drew alone for a second. He and Dad can go watch a movie, but to suggest he sees Dad's coin collection is just silly."

Harold stood up and adjusted his pants to rest perfectly on his waist. "Mel, leave your mother alone." Harold chuckled. "Come on, Aaron. We can go to my man cave and watch a movie, play pool, or I can show you my coin collection if you really want to see it." Harold rubbed his hands together in glee. He looked to Aaron and then looked at Melanie before his shoulders shook from his hearty laugh.

Melanie didn't find him funny.

Aaron squeezed Melanie's hand as he whispered in her ear. "It's okay. Your dad is cool. Plus if I let him show me his coins, I'm certain it'll gain more brownie points with him." Aaron winked at her and kissed her cheek as he got up from the couch. "Alright Mr. Daniels, lead the way."

The two men made small talk as they made their way to the basement.

Marie jumped up from her seat and gathered Andrew in her arms again. She held on to him tightly until he forced her to sit down next to him. "Ma, I'll be okay." He gave her a half smile and squeezed her hand.

Melanie had positioned herself on the coffee table in front of them.

"Baby, are you okay? I know what you learned is a lot to take in." Marie covered his hand with both of hers as she squeezed it.

"You were right when you told me I didn't want to know who my birth father was." Andrew's shoulders slumped as he rested his back against the couch.

"So I take it you haven't talked to any of them yet?" Melanie asked.

"Nope. I can't." Andrew rubbed his face and pressed his lips tightly together.

"They have been calling me often. Your mom has. Your sister and brother do, too, and they text me. I haven't responded back to them and certainly won't answer for fear of talking to your dad. I don't know what I would say to him if given the chance to confront him." Melanie's nostril flared as she thought about what he did to her mother. "But they're really worried about you."

"I don't care." Andrew pulled his hand from Marie's and folded his arms across his chest. He grinded his teeth together.

"But you all are so close, Drew. You need to call them and at least let them know you're okay," Melanie said.

"Honey, I doubt that your mother knew about what your father did. I know a mother's love and what it's like to worry about a child. Don't make her suffer. Just call her and let her know you're alright." Marie pleaded with him.

Drew stood up from the couch and paced a nearby open space. He looked at no one when he spoke. "At first I didn't believe when you told me that my father, the man who had adopted me after you'd given me up, had raped you. He raised me to be a strong, intelligent man with good character, and so I

130

didn't want to believe you. But the more I remembered the fear in your eyes when you simply saw his pic. Remembering Melanie tell me how you had been over the years and seeing how many times she had to be by your side through the pain of the memories, it hit me that you're telling the truth." He threw his hands up in the air as his voice raised. "The anger and rage I have inside of me about that man is unbelievable right now. I would strangle him with my bare hands if he were here." Andrew balled his fists up and his body morphed into a Hulk-like stance as his jacket tightened around his bulging muscles and firm back. His pupils dilated and his nostrils flared. He punched the wall.

Marie walked over to him but didn't touch him. She wasn't afraid of him, but since she had never seen him like that before, she didn't want to enrage him any further with a touch. She knew some people's reactions to touches when they are enraged varied, no matter who was actually trying to comfort them. "Drew, I get that you're mad, but you have to calm down. Trust me, I know that keeping it bottled up inside is not healthy."

He turned to her. "So do you suggest I go and unleash it on him?" He spoke through clenched jaws.

"No, that's not what I'm saying." She grabbed his hand and he reluctantly followed her back over to the couch. "You see how me holding it in kept me bound for so long. It made me miss out on the best things that had ever happened to me. I ended up giving you up for adoption. I didn't love Harold the way he deserved to when we were married which led to our divorce. And Melanie was more of a caregiver to me than I was a mother to her." Marie's eyes were glossy. She sniffled.

"Aww, Ma. You were a great mother to me." Melanie squeezed her mother's hand.

"Thank you, baby." A tear escaped Marie's eye.

"See." Andrew jumped up from his seat again. "You've been crying over what that, that…" Andrew huffed. "…that nigga did to you even before I was born. He hurt you and that pisses me off. He's the reason, you weren't in my life."

Marie didn't chase after him this time. When he looked back at her and saw the sadness in her eyes, he rushed back to the couch and took her hand in his.

"I'm sorry, Ma, for blowing up in front of you. I just have no good feelings for him."

"I understand your frustration. Don't worry about me, I just need you to be alright."

Andrew looked over at Melanie who was looking at her phone. He knew she was holding back something. "What? Why are you looking like that?"

"Don't worry. You don't want to know, especially not right now." She tried her best to paste a smile on her face given the current topic of discussion and to avoid letting Andrew in on her most recent incoming text message.

"Mel, tell me."

"Well, it's your sister. She needs you to call her ASAP. She's worried about you, but also since you were the one planning your dad's retirement party and she's busy with the new baby, they need you to make sure everything is on point for it since it's coming up soon."

Andrew shook his head in disbelief. "If they think I will have anything to do with continuing to plan his party let alone be at it, they all are crazy."

"But they don't know what happened and why you're not talking to them. You have to tell them something," Melanie said.

"No, all I have to do is not see Charles the rest of my life, because otherwise, if I do, I'll be headed right to jail after I kill him."

Marie and Melanie could tell there would be no getting through to him that night.

He stood up and headed to the door.

Marie followed closely behind him. "Baby, where are you going? I'm worried about you." Her voice trembled with concern.

"I'm gone. I just need to get some fresh air."

***

Andrew sat outside of the coffee shop where he had met Renee. He needed some caffeine. Ironically it had a soothing effect on him. He wished he was going in to meet her, staring into her eyes and drinking a latte would do him a world of good. He wanted to call her but it was late and he didn't want to disturb her, especially since she seemed so different and withdrawn from him by the end of their meet up hours earlier. He needed her to hold his hand and hear her pray for him again. With that not being an option, he'd just have to settle for a grande cup of the good stuff.

He got out of his car and headed to the door and dropped his keys right before entering the shop. He bent down to get them and when he stood up, he head butted the bottom of a guy's cup causing its contents to spill to the ground. Andrew looked at the guy. "I'm sorry. My bad. I didn't see you."

"No problem. I didn't see you down there either, otherwise we could've avoided the spill." The man shook his hand off to the side of him allowing his spilled drink to drip down his fingers.

"Hey, let me get you another one." Andrew walked around the guy to open the door.

"Naw, it's okay. I'll get it."

"Naw, I spilled it, I'll buy you another one."

The guy chuckled. "Well shoot, you ain't gotta force me into letting you replace my drink. Thanks, I need this. I have a long night ahead of me."

"Okay, cool. You work nights?" Andrew asked as he made his way to the register.

The guy cleared his throat. "Uh yeah, you can say that."

Andrew placed his order with the barista and stepped aside to allow the gentleman to place his. They walked down to the end of the counter to wait for their drinks. Andrew face palmed himself as he shook his head. "My bad, I'm Andrew, and your name is?" He extended his hand to shake the stranger's.

"Marcus." Marcus could sense in his spirit that Andrew was stressed.

"One grande caramel macchiato and one clover brewed coffee ready."

"Thank you." Andrew grabbed the orders and handed Marcus his. "Nice meeting you, Marcus."

Andrew headed to a table to sit and think.

Never passing up an opportunity to minister or encourage someone as he felt led to, Marcus walked over to Andrew's table. "Mind if I join you for a second? I'm waiting on someone to call me. I was just gonna sit in my car and wait, but chatting with you for a second would probably be better."

"No problem." Andrew sat down.

Marcus quickly took his seat. His partner should be calling him soon. He wanted to help encourage Andrew if he could before he got back to his case. "So, is everything okay?" He noted Andrew's eyebrows knitting together in wonder.

Marcus smiled and laughed some. "I'm sorry, let me better introduce myself, I'm Marcus Sutherland Jr. I'm a youth pastor at my church and I work with the men's ministry, among other things."

"Okay." Andrew's shoulders relaxed.

"I'm not trying to be up in your business, but like I said, I work with the men's ministry and it's my passion to help guys as needed. I just sense that something is troubling you. I don't know if you have someone to talk to about whatever it is that you're dealing with and I know you don't know me, so you might be thinking like who is this fool? Why is he asking me my personal business? And does he really think I'll talk to him about it?" Marcus's shoulders heaved up and down as he laughed at himself. He hoped his laughter would keep Andrew at ease. He watched Andrew's face contort as if many different thoughts were floating through his mind about Marcus.

Andrew finally decided to speak. "Wow. I can't believe that complete strangers can pick up on my distress."

Now Marcus was confused.

Andrew laughed as he stared at Marcus. "You're not the first complete stranger within the past couple of weeks who's seemed to be worried about me, although she's a lot prettier than you." Andrew mumbled the last of his statement and laughed to himself.

"Yeah, well, I just wanted you to know that whatever you're going through, you're not alone. I along with some other men at my church are genuinely committed to helping one another. We vowed a long time ago to one another that we don't have time to be too filled with pride and ashamed of what we've done or what we're going through to not reach out to our brothers and lean on one another for support. We know we are the backbone of society and in order to have stable homes, stable relationships, stable kids and whatnot, we have to be mentally, physically, and spiritually stable within ourselves."

Andrew nodded his head in approval of Marcus's beliefs.

"I'm sorry if I got all preachy on you, I'm just concerned about my black brothers, all men for that matter." Marcus took a sip of his coffee and checked his watch, his partner should be checking in with him soon. "Since I've pretty much been in your business thus far, I might as well keep digging. Can I ask you something else?"

"Sure." Andrew sat up in his seat.

"Are you a believer? Have you accepted Jesus Christ into your heart?" Marcus said.

"Yup. I don't go to church every Sunday or anything like that, but I do believe that He died for me."

"Cool, one of the best decisions we could ever make." He felt his phone vibrate and knew it was his partner calling him. "It was straight bumping into you, literally." They both chuckled. "And talking for a few minutes. I have to go, but here's my card. You can call me if you wanna talk or you can meet me down at my church for the men's meetings we host weekly. Take care of yourself, man." Marcus stood up and patted Andrew on his back. He was ready to dash out the door, but he back tracked to Andrew and sat down again across from him. "I really do have to go but I would be remiss if I didn't pray with you real quick. Is that okay?" Marcus looked to Andrew for confirmation.

"Sure." Andrew extended his hand to Marcus to hold for prayer.

"We can hold hands if you want to, but we don't have to. That's the beauty of God, we can come to him just the way we are. As long as our hearts are in agreement about letting him have control over what we're praying for, then He can move. Just focus on Him real quick. Bow your head if you need to."

Thinking it was the best thing to do to focus, Andrew bowed his head.

Marcus prayed, said goodbye to Andrew again, and then left the coffee shop.

Andrew put his coffee on the table and rubbed his chin. He realized what he was going through really was showing on his face. He would have to do something about it and soon. He hoped it didn't show in the many meetings he had been conducting with his clients and the potential companies that wanted to endorse them.

He rubbed his chin one last time and a smile crept on his face knowing he had the support of Melanie, Marie, the beauty, Renee, who had seemed to make her home in his thoughts, and now yet another person was ready to be in his corner. He could call Kyle, his best friend, if he needed to, but he and Kyle never prayed together. And it seemed like prayer would be his ally. He felt a lot calmer after Marcus' prayer. He just might have to call him up from time to time or go to one of those men's meetings he mentioned. Maybe his quartet of support would help keep him sane as he

139

decided how and if he would approach his dad, his real dad, Charles. It was going to take a lot of prayer to keep from killing him.

12

Renee woke up the next morning with Andrew on her mind. That was unusual for her because the only thing she normally wanted to do when she first woke up each day was to pour out her love for God and pray as He prompted her to.

She lingered in the bed longer than she normally would and pulled the covers up closer around her neck as a sly smile widened across her face. *Andrew is fine. But I don't think he likes me like that. But wait, he called me beautiful and he smiled a certain way at me. His stare unnerves me, but he said we were just friends. Oh never mind. I have something else more important to focus on than fantasizing about him and me.* She frowned as she got out of bed. She opened her curtains letting the sunlight in, turned her worship music on, and knelt beside her bed. She prayed a heartfelt prayer leaving her clasped hands wet from her tears. "Thank You, God," she whispered as she got up from the side of her bed.

She went into her bathroom to get ready for work. Her prayers normally made her feel light and jovial as she started her day, but that morning she was still heavy and she knew exactly why. Her thoughts were consumed with imaginings of her son. One minute she was smiling thinking he was okay with the loving family he had been placed with, but in the next moment, thinking about Andrew as a grown man who was still plagued by his adoption worried her. She tried not to, but she kept wondering if maybe her son had experienced trauma from the family he had been placed with and that he was scared and lost now. She shuddered wondering if he were even still alive. Tears covered her face as she dressed for work and headed out the door.

***

"Good morning," Amina spoke to Renee as she walked past her cubicle.

Renee didn't speak but gave her a weak smile and wave as she drudged past Amina's desk headed to her office. Renee tried to shake her sadness on her car ride over but she just couldn't. She had to use Visine to get the redness out of her eyes before she walked in the building.

By the time she made it to her office and closed the door behind her there was a soft knock at her door. Renee breathed a deep sigh as she put her bags down next to her desk. She already knew who was at the door. She appreciated her coworker's concern for her, but she would much rather be alone at the moment. She spoke through the closed door. "Yes Amina, how may I help you?"

"How'd you know it was me?" Amina laughed.

"Because, I know you. Can I help you with something?"

"For starters, you can let me in."

Amina was a milder version of Kim, so Renee knew that Amina would be persistent with getting through the door and seeing if she was indeed okay. "Sure, come on in." Renee rounded her desk and sat in her roller chair.

Amina went in, closed the door behind her, and sat in the empty chair in front of Renee's desk. "Renee, I know we really only go to lunch at work and we've never actually hung out together outside of work."

Renee smiled. "Yeah, that's because you never accept any of my invitations to go to church with me."

"You're right, but that's beside the point. I may not go to church with you whenever you ask, but I do go from time to time." She adjusted herself in her chair as she stared at Renee peeling the nail polish from her fingers. "You know, I don't go to church as often as you do because I encounter God whenever I'm around you. If it ain't a scripture you're quoting or an inspirational talk with you, then it's the smile you give me. You haven't been doing either of those lately and quite frankly I feel like I'm starting to lose the little bit of religion I do have. You've got to step your game back up, girl."

Renee looked up at the seriousness on Amina's face and fell over in her chair laughing. She laughed so hard that she had to hold on to her side to squash the pain in it and wipe the tears from her eyes. "Thanks, I needed that." Her laughter had subsided.

"I'm glad I can brighten up your day, but seriously, Renee, you can talk to me if you need to. Do whatever needs to be done to get back to the happy you." Amina smiled as her tall, slender frame stood up. She smoothed out her pants and pulled on her blazer. "I'll stop in later and check on you. Okay?"

Renee gave her a half smile and nodded.

Amina left the office and closed the door behind herself.

Renee knew Amina was right. She had to do whatever needed to be done to get back happy and for her, that meant she'd have to find out about her son.

She had joy, the everlasting kind that could only come from God, but happiness had evaded her for a while. She hoped he was still named what she had put on his birth certificate because she knew once the birth mother gave over guardianship of the newborn, the courts would issue a new birth certificate to include the adoptive parent's names. She powered up her desktop and logged into the system. She had given birth to him in D.C. and here she was over a decade later sitting in Illinois looking for him. She knew her search was a longshot. Since she didn't go through a private adoption agency, but rather D.C's public process, his record was unsealed. If she had given birth to him in Illinois, retrieving his file would be no problem for her since she had access to the database, but because he was born in D.C., she didn't have access to his information.

The only thing she could do was to put in a request to their agency for his file, but that would require her to list her reason for needing the adoption files. The only legitimate reason she could think of was that she was his birth mother and wanted to check up on him. She knew that would never fly with the caseworker in D.C. She couldn't bear to have them knowing her personal life and what she had done in hopes of them doing a professional favor for her.

She began her own search. In a last attempt, she perused Google typing in what she named him at birth, but hours into it, her search yielded her nothing. She looked over at the pile of manila folders on her desk and then at the clock on her wall. She had been at work for four hours and yet she hadn't even begun to tackle the workload that she was on the clock for.

She lowered her head in her hands and cried for the rest of her work day. She needed to find her son, she just didn't know how she would do it.

***

Renee drudged across her threshold and she dropped her bags at the front door and dragged herself over to her couch, allowing her body to flop down. She was mentally and emotionally exhausted from the long and unsuccessful day she had at work. She laid there quietly contemplating her next move. The darkness that had set in her apartment after the sun had finally set and the hunger pangs rumbling in her stomach reminded her that she hadn't eaten since the bagel and coffee she had on her way out the door that morning. She remembered she had skipped lunch since she was consumed with the hunt for her son.

She sat up on her tweed couch and quickly grabbed her temples. They were throbbing. Hunger and stress must have been the recipe for the awful headache she was experiencing. She looked around her living room and nothing but the light from the tall street lamp outside her front window provided minimal light for her to see. Her fourth floor apartment wasn't the biggest, but it was hers and she was grateful for it. She just couldn't see herself living a lavish life and her son possibly be living in squalor, so she opted to live modest, but Kim called it homely.

She made her way to the medicine cabinet in her bathroom and popped two aspirin in her mouth before heading to her small kitchen and illuminating it. It took a moment for her eyes to adjust to the brightness in the room but once they did, she remembered that she had been so weighed down with thoughts of her son lately that she hadn't cooked a big pot of soup or stew like she normally did to last her throughout the week.

She walked over to the refrigerator and pulled it open and stared at its contents. Nothing but water and juice. She shook her head at herself as she opened up the freezer. There, she saw only two frozen dinners left. She would have one for dinner and the other for her lunch the next day.

She put the macaroni, Salisbury steak, and mashed potato combo in the microwave and set it to cook for eight minutes. She stood in front of it staring at the green box rotating on the flat plate inside. The longer she watched it the more intense her hunger pains grew. Time seemed to go by slower the longer she stared at it, and that frustrated her all the more.

She heard a faint sound coming from her living room. She walked to the edge of the kitchen and strained her neck into the living room hoping to better hear the noise that had now grown louder. When she realized the sound was coming from her purse, she rushed to it and snatched her phone from it. The ringing stopped but she smiled looking at the name of the missed call. It was Andrew. She touched her face realizing that it was the first time she had smiled that day since Amina had left her office. *Should I call him back?*

The microwave chimed signaling her food was ready. She grabbed her dinner and a fork and headed over to the couch with her phone in her hand. *Should I call him while I eat or wait until I finish?* She laughed at herself as she pressed the green phone button next to his name and held her breath as the phone rang the third time. It was just something about him that made her feel like she hadn't felt about a man since she'd first met Ted. She was about to end the call when she heard his voice. She put the phone back up to her ear. "Hello?"

"Hi, Renee?"

"Yeah, it's me."

"Did I catch you at a bad time?"

Yeah, a bad time in my life.

"Renee?"

"I'm here."

"I called you a minute ago but you didn't answer. I left you a voice mail. Did you get it?" Andrew sounded hopeful. He had left her a message he wanted her to hear before he spoke to her again.

"My phone didn't tell me I had a voicemail, so I didn't know to listen to anything. I'll check it soon."

"Cool. So how are you doing?"

"I'm fine." She realized that she wouldn't be able to eat and talk to him at the same time. The way her stomach tap danced like Sammy Davis Jr. whenever she talked to him or thought about him mixed with her hunger pangs didn't suit her eating at the moment. She put her food down on the couch next to her. "And how are you?"

"I'm good."

"You don't sound so good." Her legs were folded on the couch and she toyed with the hem of her skirt.

"How do you do that?"

"Do what?"

"Know when I'm lying about being okay?"

"I don't know. Of course my spirit is telling me something, but there's a despair in your voice that I'm certain wouldn't be there if you weren't dealing with what you're dealing with. Speaking of, you haven't

149

told me yet what has you so up in arms about your adoption."

He was quiet.

"Drew?"

"Yeah?"

"Talk to me."

"Okay, but not about that. I just want to take my mind off it and I want you to take your mind off whatever is troubling you."

"I told you I was fine."

"I may not be all in the spirit like you, but I hear that sadness in your voice. And I see it hiding behind your smile or eyes whenever I look into them. You can talk to me about whatever."

"You're right, let's talk about anything other than what's troubling you and what you assume is troubling me."

They talked nonstop for the next three hours. Renee never stayed up that late but she just couldn't fathom ending her call with him. They talked about everything from how they were raised, to how they dressed in high school, to their favorite movies and music, to where they wanted to be in the next five years.

"You know, if it were up to me, I would stay on the phone with you all night long, listening to your voice, but I know that you have to get up for work in the morning, so I'm going to let you get off of the phone."

Renee smiled. "Thanks, but I'll be alright if you wanna keep talking?"

"I do. But I wanna talk about what's paining you."

"Drew."

"I told you most of my story, but I know nothing about your problem. I know we just met, but I feel like we can talk to each other about anything."

Most? Her eyebrows furrowed wondering what else he could be keeping from her but she dismissed her curiosity for the time being. She sighed because she really did feel comfortable talking to Andrew, but her secret was just too much to share with anyone. "I am comfortable with you and I've opened up to you tonight in ways that I haven't with anyone in a long time." Her lips snarled thinking back to Ted. "But I'm just not ready to share that part of my past with you, with anybody for that matter." Her words trailed off.

"Okay, friend."

What? Friend again? I'm over here with butterflies in my stomach and I thought he was flirting with me at times during the call and yet he still calls me, sees me, as just a friend.

He shook his head at himself realizing that he had called her friend. He definitely didn't look at her as just a homie, but somehow in his nervousness, the word "friend" came out of his mouth. "Renee?"

Andrew noted that she was silent for a long time. If he could rewind time, he would say "Okay beautiful woman that consumes my thoughts when they are not plagued with imaginings of harming my father." But he reasoned that would be too much and too forward to say to her just yet. He was enjoying the pace that their relationship was developing. He always rushed his feelings with a woman in the past, but he knew Renee was different than any woman he had ever met before. He wanted his pursuit of her to be different. He wanted his issues with his dad to possibly be resolved because he had a feeling that she was a keeper. If he had to slow it down and not let on how he liked her just yet, so be it. He called her name again.

"Yeah."

"You were so quiet, I thought maybe you'd hung up on me."

"No," she whispered. "But I will say goodnight now."

"Good—"

She ended the call with him before he could even say "night." She knew she was maturing feelings for Andrew even though it had only been a short time since she first met him. Her interest in him was unlike what she had experienced before and she wasn't ready to battle her ever growing attraction to him. Her longing to find her son had taken first place in her heart.

13

Renee couldn't seem to make sense of her emotions lately. She had been talking to Andrew frequently and meeting him at the coffee shop as often as their schedules allowed them to. She enjoyed their face to face time. The smooth tenor of his voice, the intense way he looked at her, his smooth, chocolate skin, the humility he possessed, the way he tried to cheer her up and seemed so concerned about her well-being in spite of him dealing with something heavy in his life, it all stirred emotions she hadn't delved into since Ted. Honestly, she hadn't allowed herself to give any attention to a man since Ted.

Her traumatic experience with him and the pain of giving her son up for adoption pushed her closer to God and busying herself with missionary work, whether it be at church or on her job. Since she couldn't lean on the sisterhood for support and to help her battle her emotions because they didn't know about her giving up a baby, she didn't have anyone to confide in and encourage her about the specifics of her issue. When she wasn't with Andrew or talking to him on the phone, thoughts of how her son was fairing crippled her. To add to that, the range of cases she dealt with daily added to her being overwhelmed.

She hadn't hung out with the sisterhood in a while despite them constantly calling and texting her. She barely responded to them or answered their calls. She refused to join them for their weekly get together. They already questioned her melancholy mood, and since she had become even more somber since the last time she was around them, she knew if she was in the same room with them, they would poke and prod at her until she fessed up. Just last week Kim had busted through her door demanding she come clean about whatever she was going through. She thought she did a pretty good job of putting Kim's fears of her hiding something to rest, for the time being.

With Pam recently revealing that she had an affair with a married man, but they still loved her back to life, and how they always put up with Kim's shenanigans, Renee knew deep down that they would eventually support her decision surrounding her son. However, she knew the reality of her not telling them any aspect of her secret over the years would hurt each of them to the core. That was not a pain she was ready to inflict on their friendship, plus she still didn't know exactly what she was going to do with her growing desire to find her son.

It was nearing the end of the day and she sat at her desk scrolling through the minimal pics she had in her picture gallery. Her heart melted when she stopped at a pic of the twins. She hadn't seen them in a while. She missed them and maybe kissing their chubby cheeks and hearing their tiny laughter as she played with them would do her heart some good.

Since she had encountered Kim last week and managed to evade her suspicions unscathed, she thought she would be successful with stopping by Monica and her brother, Keith's, house after work.

***

Renee stood at their door ringing the bell. She had a key to their house but would never invade their privacy the way Kim so easily did each of them. She had texted Monica asking if it was okay for her to stop by after work to see the twins. She was all the more relieved when Monica told her she wouldn't be at home because she had an event to tend to that night, but Keith would be at home and she would notify him.

"Hold on," Keith yelled out from the other side of the door. He finally opened it with his daughter backwards under his arm and gave a brief smile to Renee before he went running after the other one rapidly teetering away from him. He scooped up his son under his free arm and ushered Renee into the den. He put them down on the alphabet tiled rug and pushed some toys in front of them hoping the gadgets would occupy the twins while he talked to Renee.

She picked up her niece and began tickling and kissing her, relishing in her joyous laughter.

She finally looked up at Keith to see him staring intently at her.

"What?"

"Don't what me." He got on his knees and smothered her in a hug.

"Keith, your baby. Don't hurt her."

"I won't. She's on your lap." He finally released her and sat back down on the floor directly in front of her.

"Why have you been ignoring us?"

"I haven't been ignoring anyone." She refused to look him in the eyes, but instead looked down at her niece playing with the zipper on her jacket.

She heard noise coming from the back of the house but ignored it assuming maybe it was the TV on in the media room.

157

"Yes you have," he said in a deep, authoritative voice. "I didn't know what Ted was doing to you in college until after the fact. Mom and Dad talked me out of coming to your rescue then, but with the ladies constantly talking about how you've been avoiding them and me not seeing you across the dinner table many a Sunday at Mom and Dad's, I've seriously been figuring out how to hurt dude without jeopardizing my freedom and my family's future. I've sat outside of your apartment building a few times thinking that if I walked in on a dude hitting you, I would kill him. I was going to bust down your door the day Kim did, but Monica talked me out of going. She knew where my head was and that I wouldn't be rational if I found you in a bad way."

"Why is everyone thinking I'm in some abusive relationship again? I'm not even in a relationship right now." Her mind drifted to the friend zone status they seemed to be in.

"Because they say this is the same way you behaved when you withdrew from them in undergrad."

Renee shook her head as she freed her niece's wiggling body from her grasp. She headed to play with same toy her brother was playing with. They began to talk in jibberish. "It's not the same though. When I was going through what I was going through

158

with Ted, I had no communication what so ever with them. I text them back when I can."

"What has you so busy though, sis, that you don't have time for family? For the sisterhood? Mom? Dad? Your niece and nephew? Me? You're big on family, this is so unlike you."

"Keith, I promise I'm fine. It's just work."

Keith eyed her for quite some time trying to gauge if she was telling him the truth. The shiftiness in her eyes and the tenseness in her body let him know that she wasn't being totally honest with her, but he decided to leave her be for the time being knowing the sisterhood would get the truth out of her soon enough.

He stood to his feet and then reached down to pick the twins up.

"Hey, where are you going with them? I came over to see them." Renee's eyebrows knitted together in confusion.

Keith laughed as the twins dangled from each of his arms. He looked down at her. "I know you did, but there are people here to see you." He walked away.

"People?" Renee jumped up to her feet although her attempt was not as rapid and clean as she would have liked to be. She stepped on the inside of her ankle length skirt causing her to trip and fall to her knees. "Who? What people?" she called out to him as she remained on her palms and knees.

"Us," Monica said as she, Pam, and Kim appeared in the entryway on the other side of the staircase that separated one side of the house from the other. They walked towards Renee helping her to sit down as they saw her gearing up to head to the front door.

Renee's eyes bulged at Monica. "You told me you wouldn't be here tonight."

"I was thinking about tomorrow night when I responded. Once I checked my calendar to see that I had my dates mixed up, I didn't bother to tell you. I figured since you were coming over we could have an impromptu girls night since you've been M.I.A. for all of the other ones."

Renee's nostrils flared as she shot Monica a deadly stare.

"Ha!" Kim high-fived Monica. "I see I've taught you well, grasshopper."

Everyone laughed except for Renee.

"Seriously, Renee, we miss you." Pam pouted as she sat on the arm of the chair they had forced Renee into. She wrapped her arms around Renee's neck and held on for dear life.

Renee didn't flinch.

"That's okay. You don't have to hug me back, just take all of this love I'm showering on you." Pam giggled and kissed Renee's cheek before she walked away from her and took a seat on the couch across from Renee.

Monica still stood brooding. "I would hug you but I'm so mad at you right now." Her eyebrows crinkled as she pouted at Renee. She looked at Renee for a bit longer before she gave in. "Oh, you know we can't be mad at each other for too long." Monica ran towards Renee before throwing herself on her.

Renee fell back completely in her chair under the weight of Monica's toned body. "Monica, get off me. I can't breathe. You're acting crazy right now like Kim." Renee's chest heaved up and down trying to get new air in her lungs since Monica had knocked the wind out of her when she fell on her.

"Oh hush, you'll be fine," Monica said as she gathered herself off Renee. She, too, kissed Renee's cheek before she backed away from her.

"So, she can be crazy, too, when it comes to being up in your space." Kim's stare dared Renee to object to the notion as she walked past Renee and sat on the floor near her chair.

Renee stared at each of them briefly before she spoke and directed her words at Monica. "You know you didn't have to trick me into coming over here. You could've just told me you all wanted to see me." Renee adjusted her twisted clothes on her body.

"Uh ha." Kim made sure her maniacal laugh belted throughout the living space. "We've been doing that all along and you hadn't showed up yet. Trickery was the next best thing."

Pam and Monica shook their heads and smiled.

"Whatever." Renee sighed, exasperated.

"So, chica, long time no see. What's really going on?" Monica asked finally flopping down on the couch next to Pam.

"Nothing new. Just busy with my caseloads." Renee hated that all of their eyes were fixated on her. It was as if they each had magnifiers for eyes and trying to examine every part of her to see if she was lying to them. She looked away from them and over to the unlit fireplace. She wished it was lit so she could stare at the flames and that the crackling of the embers burning could drown out the eerie and uncomfortable silence of them staring at her.

"Renee?" Pam spoke loudly trying to regain her attention.

Kim looked up at Renee and shook her head. "Unh hunh, you're holding that same far off look and zoning out on us that made us question what's up with you before you did your recent disappearing act."

"Whatever, Kim. Aren't I allowed to get lost in my thoughts from time to time?" Renee stared directly at Kim.

"No. You never used to do that. You were always present in every moment, listening to everything we said and watching everything we do, ready to compare it to the word of God and let us know when we're not lining up with it. Where'd that Renee go?" Kim raised one eyebrow as she stared back at Renee.

"That Renee calmed down. She's gotten closer to God and realized it's just better to pray about stuff than to put her mouth on it." Renee spoke about herself in third person.

"Well people don't just up and change their character like that unless there's some life-altering, traumatic event that causes them to do so." Kim hoped her catty response would bait Renee into fessing up what was going on with her.

"Well then I'm waiting to hear you share what caused you to go from being just as much of a prude as I was before college to pretty much being a harlot after we graduated." Renee didn't back down from Kim this time. Too much was on her plate mentally to take anymore worry from Kim.

Kim's big round eyes bucked wider than they normally were and her head cocked back as she balled her fist up and raised it in the air. She narrowed her eyes in on Renee and tightened her lips as she spoke. "If you were anyone else, I would clock you right on the mouth for coming at me like that, but since I'm used to you being judgmental and calling me variations of a harlot, I'll let it slide. Welcome back, sis." She smiled and buckled over in laughter on the floor.

Pam finally exhaled and Monica sat back on the couch again after they had suspended their breathing in shock, hoping that the sisters vehemently staring one another down wouldn't indeed throw blows at each other.

With a wary snarl curving her lips, Renee stared at Kim rolling on the floor still reeling in her laughter. "You really are crazy." She spoke loudly over Kim's continued laughter, "Ladies, before you ask me again for the millionth time, I am fine. All is well with me." She sat up straight and plastered what she hoped would register as a genuine smile on her face. "You're right, I haven't been around lately and unfortunately if our case load volumes don't lighten up soon, I still won't be physically present with you all for a while."

Kim was now sitting up again. Her laughter had subsided and was replaced with an inquisitive look as she stared at her sister. She needed her triplet spidey sense to kick in so she could filter through her sister's words and body language, but to her dismay, it hadn't kicked in yet.

Renee ignored Kim's unwavering stare at her and continued on. "But since I'm here, let me catch up with everyone else. How is your mom recovering after the fall and surgery?"

Kim's round face softened as she turned her attention to Pam. They all did.

Pam smiled. "She's doing great, except for the chronic headaches she has at times."

"Oh wow. Have the doctors said why she gets them?" Renee asked.

"Just the aftermath and healing of her brain. They have lessened since they started and the doctor said she shouldn't have them anymore once her healing is complete."

"Great." Renee smiled, genuinely happy that time. She knew just how scared Pam was when her mother fell the year before causing her to have a seizure and the doctors had to perform an emergency surgery to stop the bleeding and swelling on her brain.

"You would know exactly how her mom is doing if you wouldn't avoid us so much." Kim hit Renee on her knee.

Renee ignored Kim and continued to catch up with Pam. "So are you all still in a good space with your mother daughter relationship?"

"Yup, she's not bullying me anymore."

They all laughed interrupting Pam's speech.

"She never bullied you, she was just very overprotective of you," Monica said, chuckling.

"No, Eilene Robinson was and definitely still is more of a bully than just an overprotective parent. Now she makes sure that Vance and I come over for Sunday dinners whenever we haven't planned to go to his brother's house for dinner just so she can fill the evening with her new line of questioning for us. 'How soon will you marry Vance? And when will y'all start making babies?'" Pam mocked her mother down to her hand gestures and voice. "She has bridal magazines out and all during our chats after dinner."

"My parents know not to ask me about getting married." Kim's face was stoic as she leaned back on her elbows on the floor.

"Yeah, you say that now, but I'm telling you, when that one comes along, you'll definitely sing a different tune." Monica cocked her head at Kim.

Kim looked to Renee waiting to hear a word from the Lord via Renee, but Renee remained quiet. Kim's eyebrows creased as she spoke. "See, something ain't right with you. You never miss the chance to tell me how I should be living my life and how love will make me change. Something is definitely going on with you that you're not sharing. Trust and believe I'll get down to the bottom of it."

"Leave her alone," Monica said. "No need to ask me what's new with me, we chatted earlier. But what about you and Andrew?" Monica smiled and Kim sat

ANITA DAVIS

up and cupped her hands under her chin as she stared at Renee for her response.

Renee tried to quell the smile stirring up in her at the mention of his name. She didn't want the wrong facial expression or body language to suggest that they were anything more than friends. "We're cool. Just building a true friendship. He's easy to talk to—"

"Easy on the eyes," Kim interrupted her.

Renee tried her best not to, but Kim's accurate statement evoked that smile she was trying hard to hide.

"Yeah, I see you think he is too with as hard as you're cheesing over there. Aww, shucks now, my little sister has a crush on him. Look at that twinkle in her eyes."

Renee shook her head at Kim. "I do not have a crush on him."

"And you called her your little sister as if there is more than just the minute difference in age between you all. You three were born on the same day, the same hour, from the same womb, just minutes apart." Pam laughed.

"Oh hush. No one asked you." Kim threw one of the twins plush toys at Pam, but she ducked and it made a soft plunking sound as it landed behind the couch on the hardwood floor.

167

"I do not have a crush on him. He's just a great guy, and besides, we wouldn't work as a couple right now if I did like him. He has some personal issues he has to work through before he can be ready for a relationship."

Kim's eyebrows raised as she scooted closer to Renee. "Like what? Renee, if you see signs of him being abusive already, please run. I love you too much. I don't want to see you hurt anymore, and I don't wanna have to do life in jail for killing him for hurting you."

"While I thank you for your concern, big sister," Renee let her stare linger with Kim before she continued on, "Andrew in no way, shape, form, or fashion gives off the aura that he is a violent man. If you all must know, he's adopted, so he's found out some information about his birth mother that has really shaken him to the core."

"Like what?" Now Monica's thick eyebrows were raised in wonder as she stared at Renee.

"I won't disclose his personal information to you all, but like he said at dinner, he can't pursue a woman at the moment, I guess. Besides, I don't even think he sees me in the romantic way." Renee sighed and sank further in her chair.

"Well you're blind if you can't see that. We all agreed that night at dinner that with the way he was looking at you, he has a serious interest in you. Why do you think I tried to make that love connection for you all? Duh!" Kim stated matter-of-factly. She angled her head at Renee. "What really *is* going on with him that he wouldn't want you? I mean even though you're rubbish, being my sister alone bumps up your desirability at least five points."

The others stared at Kim incredulously before Monica threw a throw pillow at her. As usual, Kim was quick to dodge the pillow and shot Monica a look reminding her that she would win the pillow fight if Monica tried her again. The playfully battling duo's serious faces melted into smiles before Renee said, "You are ridiculous. He's just dealing with family drama right now." Renee frowned and quietly said a prayer for Andrew.

"Wow. Well I would never give a child up for adoption. Shoot, I already murdered one when I was stupid and got an abortion in college. With those dumb university doctors telling me that I was sterile after the complications from the abortion, I never thought I would conceive a child. So with what I've been through, I could never give a child up for adoption, especially not after having my beautiful babies." Monica smiled.

Kim stared them each down. "Y'all don't ever have to worry about me giving a kid up for adoption because I'm never getting pregnant." She wagged her finger and shook her head slowly from side to side adding more finality to her declaration.

Pam was the last to express her opinion. "I just can't see myself experiencing life growing inside of me and then not raise it, nurture it, love that child with all that's in me."

Tears puddled in Renee's eyes. She pretended to sneeze so that she could run to the bathroom and get tissue, when she really needed to make it there as soon as possible before the levies of her tear ducts broke and out would come an avalanche of tears flooding her face. She knew that kind of display would make her detective friends resurrect their investigation of her. She locked herself inside the teal and grey powder room and stared at herself in the mirror. *I can't come clean with them now after the looks I saw on their faces at the mere mention of adoption.* She splashed her face with water then dried it. She patted it, hoping to not make her look so drained. She just needed to make it back into the den, grab her purse, and rush home before any more talk of adoption caused her to explode in front of them.

***

Renee sat outside in her car on her quiet block. Living on the north side of Chicago, she was lucky that she had even found parking on her congested street that time of night. So many apartments compacted into small radius of blocks and yet so limited parking for the residents. She loved her neighborhood though. There were a lot of consignment shops within walking distance that she frequented when absolutely necessary. She wasn't the flashy type, didn't shop much, unlike Kim, and she also didn't mind wearing gently used closed from others whenever she did decide to add to her wardrobe. Besides, her salary as a social worker didn't permit her to live a lavish lifestyle. Granted she lived a minimal life and saved as much money as she could. She had a nice savings and had made a few investments here and there for her retirement and she never made big purchases. In fact, the only reason she went to the island with Monica for Karen and Kyle's wedding was because Monica added her and the rest of the ladies as employees to the final tab for the wedding expenses.

Her car was off and her purse was in her hand but she just couldn't manage to make her way in her house yet. She sighed knowing she left Monica's house in more despair than what she was when she got there. She hit the steering wheel in frustration. "Ugh! How am I going to find out where he is? If he's alright?" A tear fell from her eye before an epiphany reemerged to the front of her thoughts. *Vance's brother, Marcus, is an FBI agent. I bet he could help me.* They barely knew each other, but maybe, just maybe, she thought, he would actually help her.

She smiled and rushed from her car to her house to call him, but by the time she made it into her apartment, she realized the lateness of the hour. Contacting him the very next day would be the first thing on her agenda when she made it into work. She was ever grateful that that night at Marcus's house, everyone decided to exchange numbers in hopes of forging bonds before the next time they all got together. She wouldn't have to contact Pam to get Marcus's number and no one would be hip to her needing his assistance and especially *why* she needed it.

She smiled as she readied herself for bed believing that Marcus could help her along her journey when her phone rung. She smiled looking at the caller ID. It was Andrew and she was excited to talk to him although she knew she would have to mask her delight on the phone seeing as though he said they were just friends. She answered the phone and got swept away by their conversation. As they talked about many things, discovering more about each other, they each knew the other was taking their minds off their troubling woes. Talking to him comforted her until they both fell asleep on the phone.

14

"I'm so glad you could meet me here," Renee said, standing.

"Sure. How can I help you?" Marcus's eyebrows knitted together in confusion as he waited for Renee to take her seat before he took his. "I see you ordered something to drink already, mind if I grab something, too?" He stared at her as she tightly gripped her cup on the table. He could see that if she squeezed it any harder, the top would pop off and the hot liquid inside would explode all over the table.

"Sure." She looked at him. "I'm sorry I didn't wait until you got here to order, I just really needed this hot cocoa. It normally soothes me."

"No problem. I'll be right back." Marcus excused himself and went to stand in line to order his coffee and a pastry and soon he made it back to the table to see that Renee had taken on a calmer demeanor. He sat back down across from her. "So how can I help you, Renee?"

She shifted in her seat and finally relaxed her grip on her now empty cup of hot cocoa as she looked up to him. "Thank you for meeting me here. I know that you barely know me, but I need your help."

Marcus stared at Renee straight on.

"The night you and your wife hosted the party for us all to get to know one another, I overheard you telling Vance about your promotion in the bureau."

Marcus's eyes widened as he sat back in his chair.

"I'm sorry. I wasn't trying to eavesdrop, I just so happened to hear the convo on my way to the bathroom."

"Okay." His face remained stoic as he stared at her.

Renee didn't know Marcus all that well. He was very friendly that night at his house, but she was second guessing asking the straight faced, stiff Marcus in front of her to meet her.

He read the confusion on her face and decided to speak up. "No need to apologize. I believe that you weren't intentionally spying on my brother and I, it's just that no one really knows what I do. You can understand that, right?"

Renee nodded her head.

He pulled his chair closer to the table and rested his arms on it as he locked his hands together. "So how do you think I can help you?"

Renee cleared her throat and shifted in her seat. She could tell that he was an agent. His body language and stare was unsettling to her and her nerves tap danced again as her hands trembled. "Well, there is an adoption I need more info on."

"Excuse me?"

"I need help finding out who adopted a little boy."

Marcus's eyebrows and forehead crinkled as he stared at Renee.

She sensed he wanted more information from her so she continued on after taking a deep breath. "I haven't admitted this to anyone, but I suspect you won't help me if I don't give you the full truth." She took another deep breath and willed herself to finally share her secret with someone. "I got pregnant when I was in undergrad, but instead of having an abortion as I lead my friends to believe, I carried the baby to full term and gave him up for adoption to keep my abusive boyfriend from ever hurting him." A tear spilled from her eye.

His shoulders relaxed as he watched Renee try to keep it together. "I'm sorry that you've had to go through all of that. I can only imagine how it's affected you." He watched her try to steady her trembling hands under her armpits. "But what do you expect me to do?"

She unfolded her arms and wiped her face of the tears that had settled on it. "I don't know if you remember, I know we had minimal interaction that night, but I'm a social worker. I work with the department of children services. I investigate reports of abuse of kids in foster care. I have clearance to access adoption files here in Illinois, but my son was born in D.C., and I can't access his records."

Marcus rubbed his chin and nodded his head with a somewhat better understanding of her dilemma. "Why can't you just call in a favor to the D.C. department?"

Renee hesitated before speaking. "To ask for pertinent info from the file would require me to tell them why I need it and I can't bear to tell them my personal business, especially not what I just shared with you."

Marcus reached out and patted her hand for comfort as tears drenched her face again.

"Truthfully, you're the only person that knows my secret." She lowered her head as she stifled her cry.

Marcus wrung his hands together. "Renee?"

She looked up at him.

"Again, I'm sorry that you had to go through all of that and keep it to yourself. I don't want to sound insensitive with my question, but how do you think that I can help you?"

Renee wiped her face as she looked back up at him. "Well, I figured since you're in the bureau, you can access any files that you want to..." She stalled before speaking again. "So I figured you might be able to access his adoption records and give me info on him?"

Marcus scooted to the end of his chair and lowered his voice as he spoke to her. "Again, not many know where I work and what I do, and those who do know that I wouldn't jeopardize my job or reputation fulfilling family and friends requests. I would never abuse my privileges at the agency." His tone was curt as he spoke but seeing her tremble as he finished his statement made him soften his facial features in hopes of putting her at ease.

"I'm sorry for even asking." Tears streamed her face. She had become so fragile in his presence.

He sighed loud and deep as his back fell against the chair and he let his hands fall into his lap. "I'm sorry if I sounded too harsh with you, it's just that—"

"No, I understand." She sat up straight and wiped her face. "I was just going along with the whole 'ask and you shall receive, knock and the door shall be opened' faith logic. You don't know me, so I get why you wouldn't be willing to help me let alone jeopardize your standing with the bureau. It's good to know that you are a man of integrity. I try to be a woman of integrity as well. Honestly, I doubt if I would help someone who came to me asking me to check records I have access to. I like my job and the reputation I have with it." Renee was rambling on so that she didn't even notice the big smile Marcus wore on his face until his soft chuckle alerted her. Her eyebrows furrowed as she stared at him in confusion. "What?"

"The scripture you quoted. I often say that to the men I minister to when I'm encouraging them to press beyond the circumstances they feel are holding them back from getting what they want." Marcus rubbed his knees as he stared at the long line of people waiting to order their drinks.

Renee nodded. "Again, I'm sorry for asking you. I understand that you can't." She stared past him at nothing in particular.

"You know what, I'll help you. Your request should go under the radar."

Renee's face lit up with hope and joy.

"But I need you to make sure that you don't share with anyone, not even your best friends, that I'm an agent. Agreed?" He titled his forehead and raised one eyebrow.

"Certainly." Renee's smile was wide and bright. She lowered her voice before speaking again. "And can you please not share my secret with anyone? I mean no one."

"Of course." He nodded his head. "Your business is your business."

"Thank you so much." She squeezed his hand in gratitude. "Here is the info that I do have on him. Hopefully it's enough to help you find him."

He looked down at the paper she handed him. "It's enough. I'll call you as soon as I find out something. Let me get out of here. I have to head to church for a men's meeting."

"Okay. Thanks again."

Marcus left the coffee shop.

Renee got up from her table en route to the bathroom to freshen her face before Andrew arrived since they agreed to meet there for coffee.

***

Andrew was a few storefronts away from the coffee shop when he saw Marcus leave it heading to his car. Had he not been so far away from Marcus and so eager to get into the shop to see Renee, he would've caught Marcus's attention to say hi. Marcus had proven to be a good sounding board for him. Marcus called him often checking up on him and praying with him. The conversations were cool as long as Marcus didn't ask when he would make things right with his dad. That question always enraged him. His talks with Marcus, his visits to the men's meetings at Marcus's church, his commitment to his clients, and getting to know Renee whenever they talked or met at the coffee shop, helped him to keep his mind off his dad. It all comforted him while ignoring the continued calls from his adoptive mom and his brother and sister. Besides, he could hold off on talking to Marcus in that moment, because if his time with Renee ended early, which he hoped didn't, he would run over to the church and catch the end of the men's meeting.

He smiled to himself thinking that the coffee shop Renee had first introduced him to really was popular. He met her there often and it was where he first met Marcus, two of the people he'd been talking too often.

He walked into the coffee shop at the same time she was headed toward a table. *She gets more beautiful each time I see her. And she has a certain glow about her tonight.* He smiled and rubbed his hands together in excitement as he made his way over to her table. "Hi, Renee." He smiled as he stood next to the table.

"Hi, Drew." She smiled as she looked up at him. She remained seated. She really didn't know how to behave around him when it came to them greeting one another hello or goodbye. Since he had made it clear from their first lengthy conversation that they were just friends, she didn't dare want to hug him and lose herself in him. The sporty cologne he always wore intoxicated her senses from across the table, so she could only imagine how he would smell if she laid her head on his chest as he wrapped his defined arms around her in a hug.

She hadn't been in a man's arms since the last time Ted held her body after he beat her up. Nothing about Andrew reminded her of Ted. She felt safe with Andrew and knew that she could easily unravel in his muscular arms.

She found herself staring at the ripples and waves of his biceps at times as she sat across from him at the coffee shop. It was now fall, so he would come into the shop, sit across from her, and take his jacket off. And as customary, he had a simple, chic, fitted T-shirt on that gave her the chance to stare at his exposed arms. They would flex as he went from crossing him arms on his chest or laying them out on the table. He was animated when he talked and always incorporated hand movements into their conversations. He was the right brand of dark chocolate for her, but she worked to dismiss her attraction for him when she was around him since he had put her in the friend zone early on.

He looked at the cup in front of her. "How long have you been here? I see you ordered already. Nothing for me?" His mouth fell open as he feigned being saddened by her not ordering him something.

She looked down at her empty cup of cocoa and remembered how long ago she ordered it and why. She didn't want him to know that she had met someone there earlier and especially not the reason why. She normally didn't lie, but she needed to be quick on her feet as he awaited her response. "Um, I haven't been here too long. I was just so thirsty when I came in and kind of cold that I needed to grab something hot to warm my bones." She shocked herself at how quick the lie had rolled off her tongue. *Wait, I've lied to the sisterhood all of these years about actually having an abortion, no wonder that lie just rolled off my tongue so easily.*

"Renee, when I came in, you looked so happy, you seemed to glow, but just now, that quiet sadness of yours seemed to come back. I wish you would talk to me about it. I've opened up to you, won't you do the same?" With sincere concern in his eyes, he reached across the table and tried to grab her hand in his but she pulled away before he could touch it.

She smoothed out her long hair even though it wasn't in disarray. "I told you that I'm not hiding anything, I'm fine. Just a thought crossed my mind, but it's gone now." She waved her hand dismissively in the air.

He stared at her for a minute hoping that she would see that she could indeed confide in him whatever was troubling her, but when he saw the cloud of sadness lift from her, he retreated and decided to enjoy her while she seemed at peace. "Okay, so are you ready to eat?"

"Yup, are you treating or are we going Dutch tonight?" She laughed.

He stared at her intensely as he spoke. "You'll never go Dutch with me."

She cleared her throat and grabbed at her neck hoping to loosen the scarf around it that seemed to make her hot all of a sudden. The longer she fiddled around her neck, the sooner she realized she didn't have a scarf on. It hit her that it was the intense look in his eyes as he stared at her that made her hot. "Okay." Her throat was suddenly dry. "You know what I like, you can order for me." Her eyes bulged in embarrassment as she lowered her head and covered her face to lose eye contact with him. She didn't mean what she said to come out the way it did.

He smirked as he stood up from the table. He could tell she was embarrassed by what she said. He didn't mind it though, it gave him some inclination that she was actually attracted to him. He heard it in the vulnerability in her voice. She wasn't the overt sexy type of woman, so he knew she wasn't bold enough to say what she said in a way that hinted at something sexual. The innocence she genuinely conveyed with him endeared him and made him like her all the more.

Trying to overcome her embarrassment, she continued to look down at her outfit and shook her head with laughter. She had on another one of those outfits that Kim had snuck into her closet to modernize her look. She was grateful for it, too. She thought she saw hints of admiration in Andrew's eyes when he looked at her before he went to get their food. The taupe dress cupped her breast perfectly and accentuated her svelte waist.

He soon returned to the table with their food. They blessed it and dug in.

He couldn't help but steal glances of her as they ate. He was always pleased with what he saw. Even how she intermittently pulled at her clothes adjusting them whenever he was around her. He didn't know why she did it, but to him, it was cute.

"It's crazy how we've known each other for such a short time and yet I feel comfortable with you. I mean, your capacity to pray for me at the drop of a dime is something I will be eternally grateful to you for." He wiped his mouth with the napkin he pulled from the dispenser on the table and reached for her hand.

She let her hand linger under his touch as she stared into his eyes before she slowly pulled it away and used it to tuck her hair behind her ear.

He smiled as he sat back, noting yet again how she managed to draw back from him. He disliked that she didn't feel comfortable enough with him yet to stay in the moment and just let things flow with him, but he was confident that in time and as long as they continued enjoying each other's company as they were, she would relax with him.

"Thank you. It's my pleasure to pray for you, with you." She let the last of her statement linger in the air.

"I know we are a great duo, that's why I wish that you would open up more with me. We've told each other so much about one another. I feel like I was there with you, Kim, Monica, and Pam through it all with as many stories as you've shared with me." They both laughed, but Renee shielded her laugh with her hand.

"Don't hide your smile, it's beautiful." Andrew stared at her. She really did take his mind off everything else when he looked at her.

She smiled through tight lips. "Thank you."

"So, there's just that one bit of info that you're not telling me, that secret of yours that I think that if you share with me, you'll be freer and let your guard down with me."

Renee sighed. "I appreciate you opening up to me, but Drew, there is no big secret of mine to wait on. I'm fine. In fact, I'm more than happy." She injected manufactured joy into her voice. "Earlier today, we finalized the adoption of placing a boy I'm so fond of with a proven good family." He seemed to flow with her as she shared the details of the boys tragic past that made her so happy to place him with a loving family that day. She was grateful for the story and it being able to draw his attention away from wanting to know her secret she kept telling him she didn't have.

15

"Drew. How's it going?" Kyle asked.

"Everything's straight." Andrew fell back onto his couch making sure his beer in his hand didn't spill over.

"Dude, don't you think that I know you better than that? I can tell by that lackluster response you just gave me that everything is not alright. You still haven't confronted your dad yet, have you?"

"Nope." Andrew took a swig of the beer he was nursing.

"Why not, man? Clearly it's affecting you. You've bailed on coming out here to visit me three times since Karen and I moved here."

Andrew Chuckled. "You act like you live in another country and we haven't seen each other in years. Shoot, I just saw you at your wedding not too long ago and besides you all just moved down there to Miami. I'll get down there soon enough."

"Man, whatever. It's weird you not being down here with me this time around. Everything is so different." Kyle shrugged his shoulders in amazement of the recent changes in his life.

"Yup, let's see, when you were playing for the Miami Heat and we lived down there, your goal was to win games and get chicks, but this time around, no basketball for you. You're married, and you have a wife to keep happy, plus you have your daughter to raise."

"Yeah, I'm okay with the latter, it's just that I do miss playing and I had my right hand man here with me."

"Relax, G. I'm still your agent. I'm still helping you ink deals to keep the millions rolling in. We've been like brothers since we were little kids, ain't nothing gone change that now and moving forward, especially not the few states in between us." Andrew drank more of his beer.

"True. And because we've been friends for so long, so have our families. You know your mom and dad are worried about you and talk to my parents about your whereabouts which means my parents keep asking me about you. I know all of this is hard for you, but more and more people are getting involved because they are all concerned about you."

"Well don't answer your parents when they call like I don't answer for mine." Andrew chuckled. He knew his joke was not possible, but he wished it was.

"Man, if I didn't answer my phone everyday so they could speak to Gabby, I'd be in big trouble."

"I know! I was just joking."

"For real though, you can call me and talk to me whenever you need to. I can come up there if you like, or you could always take a break from the scenery up there and come down here. You're more than welcome in our home, but you know your way around town, too."

"Thanks, Kyle. I'll let you know if I need to take you up on that offer to stay with you and Karen for a minute, but I don't think I'll need to. I'm cool. Between Renee and this dude I met one day, Marcus, they keep my spirits up enough to maintain some type of sanity."

Kyle picked up on the little bit of excitement that Andrew inserted into his voice. "I'm gonna ignore how you've replaced me with this Marcus dude already, but I see why you won't be coming down here. You got a lady? How's it going with you and Monica's friend, what's her name again?"

"Renee. It's Renee." Andrew donned a subtle grin saying her name.

"Okay, okay, okay, Renee. I hear how you said her name. I take it you're really feeling her. What base are y'all at?"

"We ain't even made it in the ballpark yet."

"What? Drew, you don't know how to close the deal anymore?"

"I see you're still on high school stuff when it comes to women."

"Never. There was no way I could get with a sophisticated, ambitious, and intelligent woman like Karen on some high school stuff. I'm just saying, I'm the one who decided to calm my player ways. You thought you were doing that with Melanie, but we see how y'all turned out. You might be trying a different route yet again."

"Naw, you know I ain't never been a dog with the ladies and I won't start now." He smiled, thinking about Renee. "For real though, it's something way different about Renee than any other woman I've ever been with. She prays for me and with me."

"Word?"

"Yeah. You know we were raised in the church, but as I've gotten older, I don't actually go to a physical church anymore. I would say my prayers whenever the thought came to mind, but I wasn't in hot pursuit of God. When I'm around her, talk to her, think of her, I feel at peace. She's making me draw closer to God. She has something she's going through too, so instead of me focusing on my problem, I wanna help her with hers. No woman that beautiful, inside and out, deserves to deal with whatever is causing that pain I see in her eyes at times."

"Wow. That's deep. I see she's made you think about a lot. So does she know how you feel? When are you gonna step to her for real?"

Andrew chuckled to himself as he put the half emptied bottle of beer down on the floor by his couch. Suddenly he didn't want it anymore. "I haven't told her that I'm interested in her just yet because of what I'm going through. I'm not at my best and I don't want to start something with her in the middle of my troubles." He paused. "I think I want it to last forever with her."

"Andrew's in love. Andrew's in love," Kyle sang as if they were little kids teasing each other about a crush.

"Later with that. Not that there would be anything wrong with being in love with her, but I definitely am taking it slow when it comes to how I feel about her. I seriously like her though, like for real for real."

"Does she at least know that?"

"I don't know. I haven't told her flat out. I'm not sure if she's picked up on when I've flirted with her, but she is shy outside of praying. She dresses very modest." He kept quiet about so many others things he picked up on her that he liked about her. "There's just a lot to her that I like."

Kyle smirked. "Well it sounds like you more than like her, but I'll leave that alone for now. Hold on Gabby, I'm on the phone with Uncle Drew. Gabby says hi Uncle Drew."

"Tell her I said hi, too. I definitely gotta get down there and spend some time with my niece. She has to know just how cool her uncle is."

"Yeah, I want her to know you, too. I wish we could've all stayed up there, but after my career ending injury with the Chicago Bulls, Gabby's mom, Mercedes, decided she wanted to move back here to Miami, it was either I stay in Chicago with the love of my life, Karen, and be a summer only dad to Gabby or do as I did and move down here to Miami to be close to my daughter," Kyle said.

"Yeah, I'm just glad that when Mercedes did show up after three years of not telling you about your daughter that she didn't want anything more from you other than to be in Gabby's life"

"Shoot, me, too. You were there. You know how hard I had to work to prove to Karen that she and I belong together in the midst of her stupid ex fiancé Dennis paying women to lie and say that I fathered their children."

"Yeah, dude was straight thirsty for Karen," Andrew said, reflecting back on Dennis's deception where Kyle and Karen were concerned.

Kyle chuckled. "Who wouldn't want my Karen? She has it all. But I'm just glad that in the end, the women came forward and told Karen how Dennis paid them to lie. And since Mercedes and I never was in a relationship, it's easy for us to co-parent Gabby and Karen see that Mercedes is not a threat to our love."

"You sound so in touch with your emotions, 'our love!'" Andrew laughed as he held up air quotes mocking Kyle.

"Whatever. I'll be that way about Karen. She's worth it. And from the looks of it, Renee will have you all starry eyed, too I'm sure I'll return the jokes on you when you bring her down with you."

"We'll see about that."

"Right. But I gotta go. Gabby has been begging me to have this tea party with her. I'll holla at you soon."

"Okay. And I know you want to play tea party as much as she does. Bye, man." Andrew ended the call before Kyle could bad mouth him.

He put his hands behind his head and propped his feet back up on the ottoman in front of the couch. He was in a better mood now than he was before he started his conversation with Kyle and he knew it was because he spent the last of it talking about Renee rather than what Kyle called for—trying to get him to finally talk to his parents.

He had secured major deals for two of his clients earlier that day, that and his revolving thoughts of Renee would suffice some type of happiness for him for the rest of the day.

He closed his eyes for a moment trying to relax and soak in the peace he was experiencing when his phone rang. Oh how he wished it was Renee who was calling him but the furrowing of his eyebrows and tenseness in his shoulders was brought on by the song blaring through the speaker on his phone. It was a tune he'd designated for his sister.

He wanted to continue as status quo and not answer the phone, but conversations of dealing with past and recent wounds from the men's meetings and Renee encouraging him to deal with whatever was really plaguing him made him reason that he could at least speak to his sister. "Hello."

"Hello, Andrew?"

"Oh, baby."

195

He cursed under his breath at the sound of his mother's voice. He hadn't planned for her to be on the phone. "Lisa, I take it you're on the phone, too. Hi. Mom, hi."

"Don't just hi me, jerk. Where have you been?"

"Lisa, don't be harsh on him. We don't wanna push him away again."

Andrew could tell by the tremble in her voice that his mother had been crying.

"Well you better be glad that you're on the phone, Ma. Jerk is the nicest thing I could think to call him right now. I mean, who really ups and disappears on their family like he has? As close as we are. Look at how many months it's been since he's seen his niece." Lisa's words ceased as she coughed, choking on her tears.

Andrew wiped the tear from his eye and stalled the rest of them. He didn't mean to hurt two of the most important women in his life. "Ma, Lisa, I'm sorry if me not answering your calls or seeing you all in these last months have hurt you, but..."

"But what?" Lisa's cries had subsided and she was back to probing her brother.

"Nothing," he said.

"Oh you better have a good reason for not talking to us for this long," Lisa snipped.

"Trust me. You all *don't* want to know the truth." He walked over to the floor to ceiling window overlooking parts of Lake Michigan and other high rises along Lake Shore Drive. He leaned his head against the cool tempered glass and sighed since it seemed to assuage his oncoming headache.

"I don't know why you think we wouldn't. We've always been so close." His mother sighed a heavy breath.

"I just can't tell you all right now."

"You aren't in trouble, are you? Have you been in jail? Is that why you haven't answered our calls, you couldn't?" His mother's pitch elevated as she held her breath waiting for him to answer her.

He slowly shook his head and rubbed his now throbbing temples.

"Ma, I told you he wasn't in there. I checked all the nearby counties sites. He wasn't on record."

"Lisa, I wasn't asking you. I wanna hear it from him if he was in jail or not."

"No, Ma, I wasn't in jail."

"If you say so, but I just don't understand you keeping secrets from us and staying away. You're not pulling a Kyle and hiding from us like he did his parents when he was scared to tell them he had a daughter but not a wife, are you?"

"No, Ma." Andrew slowly made his way over to the couch and flopped back on it. He needed the conversation to end soon.

"Okay, so you won't tell us what you've been up to, but you've finished planning Daddy's party, right?"

Andrew clinched his jaws. His fists balled tightly together.

"You do know it's next weekend, right? You spearheaded it and said you would be the one to make sure he had a party fit for a king."

"Andrew, answer your sister," his mother jumped in.

He took a deep breath before speaking. He wanted to make sure he didn't disrespect his mother and sister if they forced him to answer the question.

"Andrew?" Lisa said.

He grinded his teeth together as he spoke. "No, I did not finish planning his party."

"Why not? It's next week. What are you waiting on? Did you hire someone else to finish getting it together?" The worry lines in Lisa's forehead etched deeper into her pecan colored skin.

"Lisa, no I didn't finish planning it or hire someone to do it." Andrew bit his tongue to keep from saying more.

"What do you mean you didn't? You are going to make sure everything is right, right? You know I can't do it, Andrew. I have too much on my plate with your niece."

"And you know I'm not the artsy type. I wouldn't know the first thing to do with making his party a success," his mother chimed in.

"You have to finish what you started, Andrew," Lisa commanded him. "The venue has been paid for. You told me yourself that everyone you invited RSVP'd with excitement."

"Nope. Not gonna happen. You all can cancel it for all I care."

"What? Why don't you care? Where is this attitude coming from all of a sudden? He's always been your hero." Lisa questioned her brother.

"Haaa," Andrew said.

"Why don't you want to honor him?" His mother's normally calm demeanor was being stirred into anger by Andrew's dismissive attitude towards his father.

Andrew sat up enraged. "Honor? Honor him? That man doesn't know the first thing about honor. I have to go now. Bye." Andrew ended the call despite hearing his mother and sister's pleas for help and understanding of his issue with his dad.

Lisa was still on the phone with her mother after Andrew got off. "Mom, we know neither one of us can do Dad's party the way he deserves it to be done, but there's this lady I've heard of that is a great party planner. I think her name is Monica Williams. I guess I'll call her and see if she can help us on such short notice."

***

"Tuh, honor." Andrew was up to his one hundredth push up trying to blow off steam. With the way he felt, he probably would do a thousand and he would still be just as pissed off with his dad. He would do jumping jacks then. He threw his phone on the couch after he ended the call with his mom and sister so he didn't hear his phone ringing. He was in no mood to talk to anyone, but as his phone continued to ring, the ringtone registered to him as Renee's. He took a deep breath trying to shake off his mood she would probably sense. He always felt better after he talked to her, so he needed to hear her voice. Maybe she'd pray for him, too.

She heard him say hello right before she was about to end the call. "Drew? Did I catch you at a bad time?"

"No. Why'd you ask that?" He got up from the floor so quickly that his headache seemed as if it pierced his brain, forcing him to ball up on his knees momentarily.

"Drew? Drew? Are you there?"

"Hold on," he said in a faint voice as he stretched, holding the phone out in front of him. He soon found the strength to stand up and head to the kitchen to get some water.

"Hold on, Renee, just hold on a little longer please."

"Okay."

After downing a bottle of water, he said, "Okay, I'm back."

"Is everything okay?" she asked.

He heard the worry in her voice. "Yes, I'm fine, lady. I was just working out and when I got up from the floor to talk to you, the blood rushed to my head too fast. Plus, I have a headache. I guess it was too much for my senses at the moment."

"Okay. Well I hope your headache goes away soon."

"Thanks."

"Other than that, how are you?" she asked.

"You always manage to make me a priority in the conversation rather than yourself."

"No I don't. I told you I'm genuinely concerned about others."

"Yeah, but I wish you would turn that concern to yourself and really deal with what you're trying to hide."

"I keep telling you I'm not hiding anything." She shifted in bed.

"Yes you are hiding something. You might think you're doing a good job with hiding it from me but you're not. I might not know why just yet, but I bet I will in due time. I really am here for you whenever you're ready to talk to me."

Renee blushed but dismissed the fuzzy feeling overtaking her. She wanted to remember that he had already declared they were just friends, so any concern he had for her was strictly platonic. He didn't push her any further to speak about the matter and she was grateful for that. She shared how her day went and answered other questions he asked.

He told her about his day and the deals he secured for his clients but left out the conversation he had with his mom and sister.

"You know, we've been chatting long enough for me to recognize some things about you," he said.

"Oh really. Like what?"

"Well yeah, you've been engaged in our convo tonight, but I do detect this edge in your voice. I don't know, like you're antsy about something."

"Drew, I'm telling you it's nothing. I do need to get some sleep for work tomorrow though, but I'll see you at the coffee shop later in the evening, right?"

"For sure. Goodnight."

"Goodnight." She ended the call. She had called him to help get her mind off meeting Marcus the next day, but with him saying she seemed on edge and was hiding something from him, her nerves remained at an all-time high. She laid in her bed with all of the lights off but sleep evaded her until the wee hours of the morning.

16

Renee sat at the table she had become accustomed to sitting in with Andrew on their "coffee runs". Neither one of them had mentioned a romantic interest in one another. She was okay with that for now, maybe forever. He was proving himself to be a good friend and he definitely kept her mind off her son when they were lost in conversation.

Her newly formed fidgeting habit she had fell into since she decided she wanted to find her son and her budding interest in Andrew left her sitting at the table tapping her fingers and knocking her knees together as she waited for Marcus to show up. From his tone of voice over the phone, she couldn't detect whether he had good or bad news for her, but she needed to know whatever it was he had to share. Her knees continued to knock together as she bit her fingernails. None of the chatter of patrons nearby nor the sounds of the espresso and coffee machines whistling interfered with the what-ifs storming her thoughts. All she heard were the loud thumps of her heart beating with anticipation for Marcus' arrival. It seemed as if her heart was beating in her ears as she looked up and saw him enter into the coffee shop. With wobbling legs, she stood up and signaled him over to her table as she saw his head rotate and his eyes scan the shop for her. She held on to the table for support. The blank expression on his face as he walked towards her did nothing to comfort her frayed nerves.

"Renee." Seeing that she was trembling, he put his arm around her shoulder as both a greeting and a means to provide her some comfort. "Let's sit." He motioned for her to take her seat again.

"No. I don't want to sit. I just need to know what you found about my son." Her stare was fixed on the brown clasped envelope Marcus held in his hand.

"Okay. This is what I have for you so far." He held out the envelope for her to take.

Renee grabbed the envelope and quickly unlatched the clasp as best as her trembling hands could steady themselves. She took a deep breath before she pulled its contents out. Her ability to breath ceased as she stared into the face, into the eyes, of a little boy who looked like her brother, Keith, in so many ways. She and Keith favored each other more than she and Kim did. The more she looked at him the more she realized that he looked like the male version of herself. She lifted the papers in her hand as it registered to her that the water saturating the papers were from her tears. She hadn't breathed in what seemed like forever and when she opened her mouth to exhale, a muffled, screeching, whimper escaped her lips but she quickly cupped her mouth. She didn't care if others heard her or stared at her as tears flooded her face, but having her hand up to her mouth seemed to be the only thing stabilizing her body from collapsing. In the surveillance pictures that Marcus's friend in D.C. captured, the boy was caught laughing as he threw a football to one of his friends on his block.

Marcus decided to speak amidst her speechless array of emotions. "Renee, once you look through the papers, you'll see that I discovered he's with a great family and he seems to be well adjusted."

Renee was elated that he hadn't seemed to suffer the same heartbreaking fate as many of the kids she'd placed over the years, but then it hit her just how much of his life she had missed as well as wanting to be a part of his life now. The only way she was able to express herself in that moment was to whimper as her body trembled with the realization that she had finally seen her son, at least a picture of him, after longing for him for so many years.

Hating to see her as she was, Marcus pulled her into his arms.

No one but Marcus knew what she was going through. It seemed as if the action of him putting his arms around her and being there with her, for her, caused her to tremble and cry all the more as she encased herself in his embrace and cried on his chest.

***

Andrew was full of excitement moments ago with the thought of seeing Renee, but now that he stood in the doorway of the coffee shop and stared at her wrapped in his new friend's arms, he didn't know what to think. Confusion, anger, and jealousy warped his thoughts as he stared at them embracing one another. The woman and man who he'd been leaning on and confiding in as of late and who had been praying for him were having an affair with each other. *Does she even know he's married? No wonder she hasn't talked about an "us", she's too busy with him.* He backed out of the door and headed back to his car. It was good that he had abandoned the idea of confronting them right then and there. The rage of his father's actions towards his mother and the fresh betrayal of his two new friends was battling within him. He knew he would be explosive to anyone who crossed his path. He needed to be alone.

***

Renee was so overwhelmed with her emotions after getting the information on her son that she completely forgot that she was supposed to meet Andrew at the coffee shop. Marcus walked her to her car and she managed to drive herself home. She crashed from exhaustion on her couch as she cradled the eight by ten image of her son.

17

"Where is your brother?" Elizabeth, Andrew's adoptive mother, craned her neck scanning the room looking for Andrew.

"I don't know, Mom." Lisa responded to her mother.

"Well did you call him again like I told you to?" She smoothed out her black dress with sparing silver sequins.

"I did, but he's not answering. He may not show up after all like he told us he wouldn't." Lisa looked across the room to see her husband holding their baby. She smiled. She was trying her best to keep her mother calm and find Monica to again thank her for how swiftly she was able to get the magnificent party together. Before abandoning planning the party, Andrew had contacted the university his father was retiring from and managed to secure a space for the party. The room given to them for the night was elegant and adorned with ornate bookcases filled with treasured texts and academic awards the school had won over the years, a few his father had helped the school to win. The room was befitting for the night and the guest of honor.

So getting a venue was one less thing Monica had to do, but she did find out that was pretty much all Andrew did on his planning efforts. He hadn't secured caterers nor a staff to serve the guests. So along with that, she had to plan the menu, format the program, and contact people to speak to honor Charles' illustrious career. Not only was he a notable professor across the country but he had written chapters and portions of so many textbooks and resources used in classrooms and curricula across the world that his intellect and contribution to education and teaching would carry on long after he retired and succumbed to death for that matter. Andrew hadn't planned for a theme for it, but with a distinguished reputation such as the honoree, Monica thought it would be wonderful to make it a black tie affair. She was successful in procuring the guest list from Lisa, since helping Andrew compose it was her only contribution to the early stages of planning it, however, Monica had to contact all of the guests and get them to agree to wear black tie attire. As she looked around the room seeing all of the women looking beautiful in their evening gowns and the men in their tuxedos, she was pleased. Cocktail hour was ending and every one would take their seats at the round tables decorated with white linen and bold silver and black centerpieces. There wasn't much else that Monica needed to do to decorate the space. The black and white sculptures resting on pedestals throughout the room she brought in made the tables and theme of the night tie in perfectly with the high ceilings and hand carved columns situated sparingly throughout already clothing the room.

"Ma, everything will be alright. We have to go take our seats. I see Monica introducing Kyle's dad to speak." Lisa scanned the room again as she escorted her mother to their table. She still didn't see Andrew anywhere and she frowned not seeing Melanie and her mother either. She was privy to Andrew and Melanie's true relationship with one another and she agreed that it would be hard for her, too, to get past dating her brother, even if she didn't know he was her brother as did Melanie and Andrew.

She helped her mother in her seat and kissed her dad on his forehead before going to take a seat next to her husband. She immediately grabbed their baby from him and snuggled her close to her body. She knew she would have to excuse herself soon to go and nurse the baby.

"Hello everyone. The family asked me, his oldest friend, to stand and share some stories of this remarkable man. Well since I don't have any of those, I'll just tell you what I do know about him."

The crowd laughed as Kyle's father recounted a few stories of Charles Sr.

***

Andrew sat in the parking lot of where his father's retirement party was being held. Elizabeth, Lisa, and even his brother had left him countless messages that day. None of which he returned, but the last pleading message his mother had left compelled and convicted him to at least show his face there for her sake, but he knew he had every mind to confront Charles as well, if prompted.

His anger was at an all-time high. He was confused. He was vexed over what he assumed was Renee being with another guy, not to mention it being Marcus, his new, married friend. He was tired of feeling the way he had been and decided that the party might as well be a good of a night as any to say something to Charles if it came down to it. Everyone in attendance held his father in high esteem, so he figured it would serve Charles right to have his pedestal yanked right from under him in front of those who admired him the most. He felt it would be some type of recompense for silent humiliation and turmoil Marie suffered through for years.

***

"Many of you all have encountered him in the academic arena, but I stand here to introduce him as the best husband a woman could ever ask for and the best father children could ever have. Ladies and gentleman please help me welcome my husband to the stage, Charles Dodson Sr." Elizabeth smiled as everyone stood from their seats and applauded him until he took the stage. He gave her a lingering peck on the lips, then nodded his head and lowered his raised hand in the air encouraging everyone to be seated.

The applause finally subsided and Charles cleared his throat to speak.

Andrew snuck in and sat in the seat wedged between his mother and sister. Elizabeth' eyes welled with tears as she squeezed his hand. His sister nudged him in the side as she whispered to him. "You better be glad you came."

Andrew looked around the table and nodded his head at his brother and his brother's wife as well as his sister's husband.

His father speaking up caused him to snarl as he lowered his head. He wouldn't dare look at him.

"I would first like to thank my wife, Elizabeth Dodson, my daughter and her husband, Lisa and Stanley Colfax, my beautiful granddaughter, Ariel, and my sons, Charles Dodson Jr. and Andrew Dodson who just arrived late to the party. You all know him, the sports agent was probably at a meeting somewhere making millions for his clients."

Some of the audience laughed.

Andrew was fuming. He didn't want the man to utter his name. Sitting in the same room, breathing the same air with him for the first time since he found out what Charles did to Marie disgusted him more than it ever had up to that point. He didn't need to look into Charles's face to see why Marie gave him up for adoption, it was like looking at an older salt and pepper version of himself. He really did look just like the man. Looking at him over the years with such admiration, he had studied Charles's features many times when he was younger trying to understand how he was adopted but looked so much like him. They had the same chiseled jawline, matching thick eyebrows, broad noses, and full lips. The same deep dark brown skin. They were pretty much identical. When he finally voiced his awe to his parents, they had told him it must've been meant to be for him to be their son. Not knowing then what he knows now, he accepted the honor of looking just like his adoptive father. But now, the knowledge of the reason for their identical features made his stomach churn. He slowly turned his head towards Elizabeth to see that she bore a similarity to Marie in her facial features. Both of his mother's had big, bright eyes, small but pouty lips, full noses, and the smoothest richest caramel chocolate skin that a woman could have. He hadn't eaten in a while, but he was certain that he would throw up whatever was in his stomach soon at the sound of Charles's detestable voice.

"I am so proud of my family and all that each one of my children have accomplished." Charles Sr. smiled lovingly at his family.

"I wish I could say the same about you." He couldn't take the hypocrisy anymore and he didn't care if anyone had heard him.

Elizabeth and Lisa looked at Andrew with bewilderment in their eyes, but soon turned their attention back to what Charles was saying.

"I never imagined that over three decades ago when I started at the University of Illinois at Chicago as an adjunct professor of sociology that I would have accomplished all that I did during my career and have become the man that I am today." Charles smiled, looking out at the audience.

"Man? Man? You a man? You're the sorriest excuse for a man that I've ever known." Andrew's voice and frustration could be heard at many tables nearby.

Elizabeth leaned over to Andrew and spoke through clenched teeth. "What has gotten into you, boy? And what are you talking about?"

"Momma. I only came out of respect for you, but I need to go now, otherwise you can't blame me for what will come next."

"Andrew, what is up with you?" Lisa switched the baby to her other arm as she spoke to him with wary concern.

"You aiight, bro?" Charles Jr. normally kept to himself, but he could see the tension in his brother's face and had heard what he'd been saying since he sat at the table.

"I don't know what's going on with you but you need to straighten up now. Look, you have everyone staring at us when the attention should be on your father. You already came in here late with jeans and a button up on while everyone else is dressed up. Stop embarrassing us. Respect your father and be quiet." Elizabeth cut him a sharp look before plastering a smile back on her face and turning back towards her husband.

Andrew lowered his head and rubbed his temples as a maniacal laugh stirred in him. His laugh was low at first, but as he slowly lifted his head and slammed his fist on the table, it erupted loud within him and the room. "Haaa. Respect my father? Respect my father?" He was now standing flat footed after the force of his rise caused his chair to topple over behind him. He had everyone's attention in the room by now. "Respect my father?" His lips curled up in displeasure. His eyes leaped with anger. "He doesn't deserve my respect." He slapped his chest hard. "He doesn't deserve your respect." His eyes softened as he looked to his mother but they turned deadly as he turned to the crowd and pointed at various people.

"Andrew!" Elizabeth stood and looked at him with such disappointment and yet concern.

Charles stood on stage with enough distance between him and the table where his family sat to not fully know what was going on with his son. He still tried to give his speech and pull the party goers attention away from Andrew.

Charles Jr. walked over to Andrew and grabbed him around his shoulders. "Come on, bro. I don't know what's going on with you, but let's take a walk and figure it out." Charles Jr. began escorting his brother out.

Charles continued his speech onstage, "...and I'm just so honored to know that I impacted so many people over the years. I gather from the amount of people in this room that I've touched a lot of lives."

"You got that right, you definitely couldn't keep your damn hands to yourself."

Mumbled chatter mixed with inquisitive stares at Andrew filled the room with his last statement.

Elizabeth snapped her neck back in his direction and with a deadly stare at Charles Jr. mouthed to him, "Get him out of here now." She was beside herself with anger. She and Charles Sr. had raised great kids who never gave them any trouble growing up and even in their adulthood. Andrew's recent antics, especially the show he was putting on during his father's retirement party, had raised what she knew was her blood pressure to levels she had never experienced before. Her hands trembled as she sat at her table embarrassed.

Always concerned about his children, Charles decided to cut his speech short and go check on Andrew as he saw his other son had rushed him out of the room. He didn't hear what Andrew had been saying but from the horrified look on his wife's face, the disappointed look on his daughter's face, and the chatter and curious looks from party goers seated at their tables, he wanted to see about his son whom he hadn't seen in months and had been avoiding the family altogether. "Thank you ladies and gentlemen for coming out tonight and helping me to celebrate the end of one era of my life. I hope you enjoy whatever else they have planned for the night and hopefully I get to mingle with each of you before the night is over."

A slow clap started by someone in a corner and everyone joined in until Charles exited the stage and the room with his wife and daughter on his heels.

Monica's eyebrows knitted closely together wondering what was going on. The honoree of the hour was scheduled to talk at least another ten minutes followed by a PowerPoint presentation, but since neither he or his family were in the room, she would have to alter the agenda until Charles returned. Quick on her feet, she walked up to the podium with a radiant smile on her face. "Ladies and gentlemen, please continue to enjoy your main course. We have an assortment of delicious desserts up next and in the meantime, please enjoy the sounds from one of Chicago's most talented DJ's, Mz. DJ-Tone. She'll keep you grooving as you eat and enjoy the company at your table." Monica pointed over to the DJ booth and most of the room clapped for the versatile DJ who began mixing a medley of old school hits that truly did have the participants bobbing their heads and shimmying in their seats.

***

Charles Sr., along with his wife and daughter, finally made their way to where Charles Jr. was working to calm Andrew down and trying to get answers from him.

"Andrew, what is up with you? You've been MIA for months and now you show up to Dad's retirement party, not dressed the part *and* cutting up. What's really going on with you?" Concern and confusion dripped from his tone.

Andrew stared into his brother's eyes with determination as he blocked him in the corner he was in. "CJ, move out of my way. I need to get out of here."

The tray ceilings were high, causing his loud demand to bellow throughout the hallway. Elizabeth rushed ahead of her husband and pushed CJ out of the way and slapped Andrew hard in the face. She immediately regretted it as she looked into his eyes and saw the pain behind them. She quickly pulled him into a hug.

He didn't fight her embrace.

She pulled back from him and her face was drenched with tears. She stared at him long before speaking, "I don't know what's been going on with you, but you're scaring me and your behavior tonight was completely out of line." She grabbed him up in her arms again and spoke through her tears and whimpered, "I'm so sorry for hitting you. I love you so much and I just don't understand you right now. Can you forgive me?"

He returned her embrace with strength as he squeezed his arms tighter around her. He couldn't speak just yet. He was fighting back his tears of remorse for disrespecting her with his actions, but the intense hatred he had in his heart for the man he was now staring at, Charles Sr., kept his anger brewing.

His sister came over and pulled his mother from him and draped her arms around her waist and helped her clean her face.

Charles Sr. stepped closer to Andrew studying him. He didn't know what to make of the man that stood in front of him. He didn't see one ounce of the man he had raised when he looked at Andrew. The man in front of him had his fists balled tightly, nostrils flaring, jaws clenched tight, and a distinct look of disgust for him. Andrew's stance with him didn't make any sense. "Son, what is it? You can tell me."

Charles honestly didn't know what was going on with Andrew.

"Get out of my way."

Everyone else looked to Andrew in disbelief. They had never heard Andrew use such a disrespectful tone with Charles.

Charles' face marred with confusion. He walked closer to him. "I don't know what's happened to you while you've been gone. Not sure if you bumped your head and have amnesia or something, but you better take some of that bass out of your voice and loosen up talking to me. I'm your father. You're not too old for me to handle you."

With his nostrils flared even wider, Andrew walked closer to Charles. "You can't tell me what to do."

Charles was taken aback all the more by Andrew's blatant defiance of him and inched even closer to Andrew. The two men now stood toe to toe. They could feel the heat of one another's breath on each other's faces. "I said you better take that bass out of your voice and show me more respect than what you're doing now. I'm your father, remember?" Charles' nostrils now flared.

Andrew inched even closer to Charles and stared him dead in the eyes. "And that's why I have no respect for you because you *are* my father."

"Andrew!" Elizabeth cried out in confusion and worry for her son as she saw her husband ball his fists up.

"That's right, I am your father, the one that's about to choke you up, if you don't stand down."

"Like how you did my mother?"

Charles didn't know what Andrew meant with his last statement, but he was over his son disrespecting him. He lunged forward at Andrew and pinned him up against the wall with his forearm braced under his neck.

Andrew struggled trying to free himself from Charles, but Charles had also pinned his lower body against the wall and had his left arm pinned behind him. "Let me go."

"Charles! Stop it! Let him go," Elizabeth cried out.

Charles Jr. walked over to the tussling duo. "Dad, let him go."

Andrew wriggled his body, trying to get away from Charles but Charles' daily strength training regimen and clean eating kept his body in prime shape. The adrenaline coursing his veins after his son disrespected him continued to help him overpower Andrew. He turned to Charles Jr. "Back up now. I'm the father!"

Charles Jr. obliged.

Charles turned back to Andrew. "Hear me good. I'm your father. I've never laid a hand on your mother and I will not be disrespected by any of my children. Do you understand me?"

Andrew was silent as he stared into Charles' eyes with hate.

"Do you understand me?"

"Yeah I understand you."

"Good." Charles backed up from Andrew and straightened out his suit.

"I understand you alright," Andrew said as he bounced off the wall and into Charles's face. "I see you now, the dangerous man who raped my mother."

Again, Andrew's words caused Charles to punch him with such force that it sent Andrew's body flailing to the floor.

"Charles!" Elizabeth rushed over, scolding her husband as she leaned down to help her son.

He waved her off. "That's okay, Ma." He took his time getting up as a strange bout of laughter brewed in him.

Elizabeth walked over to Charles. "What is wrong with you? Why would you punch our son?" She looked to him for an answer. She hadn't heard what Andrew had said to him.

Andrew was now on his feet and walking past his parents. He needed to go before he caused Charles serious bodily harm, but his father grabbed his arm before he could get past him. "Don't walk away from me, boy. You need to explain yourself right now." The stern bass in his voice blanketed the portion of hallway they were in.

Andrew licked his teeth, still tasting the fresh blood in his mouth from the punch to his jaw his father dealt him mixed with the remnants of the dried up blood from the slap from his mother earlier. His anger had shifted to an eerie calm as he looked at his father's hand gripping his forearm. His eyes slowly scanned the length of Charles' arm before he met his eyes. "So is that what you did to her? Said to her?"

"Boy what are you talking about?" Charles's eyebrows wrinkled in confusion as he stared at his son.

"Yes, Andrew, who are you talking about? What her?" his mother asked.

Andrew didn't face his mother but kept his stare fixed on his father. "Is that what you said to her, 'Don't walk away from me,' as you chased her around the room? Did you punch her like you punched me when she didn't give you what you wanted?"

"Andrew, you better say something to me that makes sense." Charles was confused with Andrew's line of questioning and yet angry with the venomous stare his son had fixed on him.

"Does the name Marie Sanders make sense to you?"

"No."

"Are you sure? Think again. Maybe you didn't rack that esteemed brain of yours long enough. Marie Sanders?" Andrew enunciated every syllable of her name this time.

An awareness struck Charles and he loosened his grip on Andrew's arm until his hand fell to his side. Shame and more confusion covered his face as he dropped his head.

"Yeah, that's what I thought." Andrew walked off, ignoring his mom, brother, and sister as they called after him. He walked out one door as Charles walked out of another one, ignoring his family calling after him.

18

"Hey, bro. How are you?" Marcus spoke into the phone.

Andrew had picked up the phone when he saw Marcus' number and name flashing across his screen. On one hand, he wanted to ignore the call as he did the others from Marcus, but curiosity was getting the best of him. He wanted to hear what a married man, who prayed for him all the time sounded like even though he was cheating with a woman that he just so happened to have a serious interest in. He finally decided to say something after Marcus had said hello for the third time. "Yeah. I'm here."

"You okay? You didn't come to the men's meeting this week and you haven't answered and returned any of my calls. Just checking up on ya, man."

"I'm straight." Andrew didn't bother to hide the contempt for Marcus in his voice.

"Drew, you sure you okay? You're sounding kind of bothered now. I can meet up with you now if you want to talk face to face."

"Naw I'm straight, and don't call me Drew." Andrew winced as he rubbed his jaw. It was still sore from the slap from Elizabeth and the hard blow his father dealt him. The swelling had just dissipated that morning. He sat in the dark with his feet cocked up on the ottoman. A few empty beer bottles toppled over on the floor near the couch he rested on. He hadn't been out of his house since his sparing match with his father almost a week ago. He'd taken care of his clients business via phone all week long and ignored the calls and visits of his family members.

"Okay, I've been calling you that since we first met, but if you want me to call you Andrew, that's cool, too." Marcus' eyes shifted in confusion as he sat in his car doing surveillance for his current case. "If you don't want to meet, we can just pray over the phone. You sound distressed now, but when you were coming to the meetings you seemed to be dealing better with that burden you're carrying."

Andrew dropped his feet to the ground and sat up on the couch. He was tired of Mr. "Hypocrite" trying to help him with the problem he didn't even fully know about, yet he had the nerve to be a married, cheating man. "Look, I don't wanna pray with you right now. In fact, I need to get off of the phone with you before I—"

"Hey, I don't know what's happened to you since we last spoke, but you don't have to get hostile with me. Don't worry, I won't take it personal, I know that everybody deals with everything differently. Just know that God will lift that burden for you if you let Him. There's nothing too hard for God to fix…"

Andrew rubbed his forehead and let out a long, deep sigh as he listened to what he thought was Marcus rambling on and on.

"…remember, He places people in our lives to help us, for us to help them and to be a blessing for one another. I'm here for you, if you need me. In fact, why don't you come to game night with me Saturday? You can just loosen up and relax and chill with me, my wife, and our friends. Whaduya say?"

"Naw, I'll pass."

"Well, the invitation is still yours. It's not at my house, but I'll text you the address anyway just in case you decide to come after all." Marcus saw the target he needed to focus on leaving a building. "I have to go, but just call me or text me if you need me, just wanna talk, and especially if you wanna pray."

229

Andrew hung up the phone on Marcus. He dismissed the last of what was said to him as he made his way over to the refrigerator to start on the new six pack of beer. His phone rang again. It vibrated on the sleek, gray toned, marble countertop. He decided that he wouldn't answer it. If it were Marcus calling him again, he might not be so cordial with him this time around and he definitely wasn't talking to his family. With the long neck bottle in his hand and half of a twist left before it fully opened, Renee's theme music for her number registered in his ear. He grabbed his phone and slid the green phone icon to the right.

"Hello." Her voice trembled.

He heard the worry in her voice and finally decided to speak. "Hey."

"How are you?"

"I'm alive."

"That's good to know." She let a weighted silence fall between them as she tinkered with the throw pillow resting on her lap. She sat on her couch in the dark staring out of her front window into the rain. With her apartment being as high up in her building as it was, she saw nothing but raindrops hitting the branches and leaves on the trees.

Her silence was too much for him. He was still brewing with anger over his father and confused about where he stood with Renee. He wondered if she really were having an affair with Marcus and whether or not she knew he was married. He still cared for her, so the worry he now heard in her voice and the pain he always saw in her eyes made him worry more about her than himself at the moment.

"Drew, did I do something wrong?" She finally decided to speak up.

You tell me. "I don't know, did you?"

She shifted on the couch to give her legs a break from being under her. They had fallen asleep and the tingling sensation hitting them was too much for her already fragile nerves.

"I mean, I've done a lot of wrong things in my life." She took a deep breath willing herself not to cry as she knew her statement was mainly geared towards her giving her son up for adoption, but she would never share that with him. "But I was asking you if I did something wrong to you to make you not answer my calls or call me for that matter." Her mouth curved down at the corners at the thought of not having talked to him in what seemed like forever. Granted she was dealing with a lot with deciding how and if she would approach her son, but talking and being around Drew had become a constant for her that she liked and had missed since they hadn't talked in days. "I've been worried about you. Are you alright?"

He shook his head and inwardly laughed to himself. He wanted to be mad at her because she was probably finding comfort with another man, but he truly cared for her. She always managed to be concerned for him. She comforted him. That always drew him in to her. "I'm as good as I can be at the moment, but you don't sound so upbeat yourself."

"I'm trying to be. I'm sorry about that night that we were supposed to meet at the coffee shop but we didn't. I got hit with some news I was and wasn't ready for. It was too much for me to take in at the moment. My emotions were all over the place. I just needed to be alone that night." She held her breath, waiting for his response. She didn't mean to say as much as she had just said. With what she said, she was sure that he would ask her specific questions that would make her have to avert his attention somewhere other than what made her so upset.

His jaws tightened. *But you let him comfort you. I wonder if he finally told her that he was married. Maybe she thought they would be together but now that she knows he's married, she doesn't know what to do. Is she just using me for the time being?* Andrew dismissed the questions swarming through his head. He just couldn't believe that the sweet, docile, and warm Renee he had come to know and care so much for would willingly be with a married man or use him for that matter. He wanted answers from her about that night, but he didn't want to add to whatever anguish he reasoned she was dealing with, so he wouldn't overtly say anything to her about it. He knew time would tell it all. "It's okay we couldn't hook up."

"No it's not. I was looking forward to seeing you that night…"

So why were you with him then? Andrew didn't ask the question out loud.

"…but like I said something came up and it wasn't until the next morning that I realized we didn't meet. What happened to you? You didn't show up?"

"Something came up." *Yeah my blood pressure after seeing Marcus cradle you the way he did. Shoot, I've never held you like that. And the way you clung to him crying as if your life depended on his arms being around you.* Andrew's nostrils flared and his breaths were short and quick.

"Drew, what's wrong? You sound mad. I can hear it in the way you're breathing."

If she were anyone else, he would let her have it, but not Renee. He felt she deserved more than to receive a tongue lashing from him and he not fully know her story. He took a deep breath to calm himself. "I'm okay. I just wish that you would open up to me about whatever is ailing you."

"You know what, we're both in need of prayer right now. Willing to pray with me?" Her thoughtfulness only made him like her more.

"Okay." He bowed his head and closed his eyes hoping to immediately go to that place of peace he found himself in when they prayed together.

"...and God we thank you for loving us so much and blessing us with what we have. We pray that your joy and peace would overtake us."

He could hear her sniffling. He wondered if she was just swept up in the prayer or crying over her burden.

"...and God please guide our steps. Show us exactly what to do in the days to come to make amends for things from our past. Forgive us of the things we've done that were contrary to your will for our lives. Help us to forgive ourselves..."

Andrew's eyes widened as he leaned on the countertop. His interest was piqued by Renee's prayer. *Is she asking for forgiveness for messing around with Marcus? So maybe she does know he's married. No wonder she can't see that I like her. She's in love with him. Of course, she ain't got time to check for me.*

"...in Jesus' name, amen."

Andrew shook his head in amazement at what he thought he discovered about Renee from her prayer.

"Drew? Are you still there?"

"Uh yeah."

"You haven't said anything in a minute. I thought the call got lost or something."

"Naw." He was mad and he needed to get off the phone with her before he said something he couldn't take back.

"Drew, did you hear me?"

"What?"

"Oh never mind. Silly of me to ask you anyway." Her shoulders slumped as she pouted.

He had been tuning in and out of the latter part of their conversation, so he didn't know what she asked him. "What'd you ask me?"

"I don't wanna go but they're forcing me to come and my sister, Kim, is insisting that I invite you to game night with my friend's and their friends."

"So you don't want me to come?" He was becoming more and more suspicious of her.

"No, it's not that. I would gladly take you anywhere with me." She quickly covered her mouth regretting her slip of the tongue.

Really? He didn't question her aloud.

"I don't wanna go, but I know my sister will literally drag me out of the house if I don't show up and if I don't bring you, they'll nag me all night about you."

Two game nights on the same night? Is this the same one Marcus invited me to? "Okay, I'll go."

"Okay. I'll text you the address." They talked for a little while longer. Their conversation wasn't as fluid as it normally was because Renee was trying to figure out if Andrew coming to game night with her was actually their first date, while he was trying to read into everything she said as admission or not of her having an affair with Marcus.

19

Sensing just how out of it Renee had been, the ladies planned game night as a ruse to bring Renee and Andrew together romantically, but they hadn't made Renee privy to that as they all mingled together in the family room at Monica's house. The twins were with Keith's parents allowing the couple to co-host the night without being on parent duty.

Andrew was there and had warily started talking with Vance and Marcus's friends Darius and Anthony. He talked with them but kept his eyes focused on Renee and Marcus. The group had just finished playing three intense rounds of Taboo and were taking a break before they started to play Catch Phrase.

Everybody was talking to someone except for Renee. Marcus saw her slumped demeanor off in a corner seat and went over to talk to her. He figured he was still the only one in the room who knew why she was so withdrawn from the crowd. He was hoping to cheer her up.

Andrew noticed Marcus and Renee in the corner talking. She hadn't said much to him that night thus far but yet her lips were moving nonstop with Marcus. He grinded his teeth as he continued to stare at them. The longer he stood there watching them talk to each other, the more enraged he became. Seeing Marcus pat Renee's hand made Andrew completely lose his cool. "Are you kidding me?" Andrew threw his hands up in the air.

"Hunh?" Darius inquired as he stood next to Andrew.

"You two have got to be kidding me." Andrew slowly made his way toward Renee and Marcus.

Monica snatched Pam and Kim up by their arms and rushed over to Renee. Monica had witnessed Andrew's outburst at his dad's retirement party, heard much of what he said in the room, and saw his bruised face before he exited the building that night. She didn't know what he was capable of doing to any of them in the room and more importantly, what was causing his new outburst.

Marcus rushed up to him. "What's going on, Andrew? You alright, bro? You need to step outside and talk for a second?" Marcus stood directly in front of Andrew. He could tell from his balled fists, clinched jaws, and the venomous stare in his eyes that Andrew was pissed, he just didn't know why.

"Man, get yo'…" Andrew flexed his biceps and paused, trying to refrain from cursing in front of all of the ladies in the room. "Just get out of my face."

Marcus's face wrinkled in confusion. "What are you talking about?"

"You know what I'm talking about. You and Renee been creeping."

Marcus' wife dropped the glass she was holding to the floor. Its contents splattered on those nearby, but they didn't bother to clean the mess or themselves up, they were still trying to take in what Andrew had said.

"Wait a minute." Marcus held his hands up in contest.

Renee made her way closer to them with a wary face. "What are you talking about, Drew?"

The sincere concern in her voice made him question his line of thinking as to whether or not he had them pegged wrong, but he thought about how his father was with him growing up versus the monster he had to be to rape Marie. Maybe Renee wasn't as naive and innocent as he thought she was. "Don't what me." He stared at her. "I've seen you two together all hugged up."

Marcus was speechless as his wife drew closer to him. Bewilderment and the onset of hurt was written all over her face.

"You can stand there and look dumb if you want to, but I saw y'all. The first time I saw you come out of the coffee shop, I thought it was just a coincidence that my new buddy, my prayer partner, was coming out of the same place I was meeting a woman that I'm really into."

Renee's eyes widened at his admission. She honestly didn't know he felt that way about her, but to find out like was too much for her.

Andrew continued on without looking at Renee. The look of confusion in her eyes was doing something to him, but he needed to get it all out. His father was the biggest hypocrite he had ever met. He wasn't going to allow any others in his personal space. No one could be trusted to him at that point.

"The very people who have been an encouragement to me lately, are having an affair with one another." He focused his attention on Marcus. "How can you preach to me about forgiveness and being the best version of myself and yet you're cheating on your wife?" He looked to Renee, who was on the brink of crying. "And you—"

"Watch it. You step to my sister the wrong way and I'll kill you right here, right now." Kim stepped in front of Renee shielding her from Andrew. The only reason she had been quiet up to that point was because she was trying to make sense of Andrew and what he was saying, but she'd figure that out later. She promised herself that she would never let another man hurt or intimidate her sister again. She'd take Andrew down on her own if she had to, but the firm grip of Darius's hands around her waist let her know she wasn't alone. Plus, Keith was now by their side as well. His stare at Andrew was more deadly than hers.

Andrew backed up some letting them know he had no plans to be physical with Renee. "I would never hurt Renee the way she did me."

Renee's face wilted into an even more confused look than what it had been since Andrew began his rant.

Andrew looked through her barricade to make eye contact with her. "You, the sweet and timid woman who calms me with prayer when I'm mad. I had you all wrong. You said you were destined to help others, well you hit the nail on the head with that one because from what I saw at the coffee shop that day, Marcus cradling your body as you cried and held onto him for dear life, you surely were helping yourself to another woman's husband. Both of you know what I'm going through and yet you betray me? Your wife." He looked at Marcus. "Just come clean with everybody and stay the hell away from me." He threw his hands behind him as he stormed out the door and slammed it behind himself.

Marcus's wife stood near him with her eyes bucked and arms folded on her chest. She stared him up and down.

Steady streams of tears traveled Renee's face. Not only was she appalled by Andrew's accusation, but the way everyone was now looking at her and Marcus for answers, it looked to her as if they thought it was indeed true.

Renee would have much rather stormed out of the house, too, but given the evil and confused looks Marcus's wife was giving him and the shaming looks of others, she knew she needed to say something, she just didn't know what.

"Is it true? You know I've never been one to jump to conclusions, but I ain't dumb either. Marcus, is it true?" His wife's voice elevated with anger and yet trembled with hurt during the last part of her statement.

"Is it true, sis? Is that why you been moping around for so long? You're messing with a married man?" Kim stared at her sister demanding an answer.

She simply shook her head at the idea of what she was even experiencing at the moment. "Renee, what's going on with you two?" Marcus's wife directed her statement and now her anger at Renee.

"Renee, you've got to make this right. If you don't, I will," Marcus stated.

"Renee." Keith called out to her.

"Aahhhhh!" Renee screamed as huge tears fell from her face and she gripped the sides of her head. "Marcus and I aren't having an affair. I would never be with a married man knowingly." She hoped that admission would be enough to simmer down the heat from everyone's stares, but the thick tension remained in the room and when Marcus's wife inched closer to her with a demanding look on her face, Renee knew she had to tell it all. "We aren't having an affair, he was helping me find my son." She covered her face in shame and ran out of the room.

20

Andrew had outed Marcus and Renee for the affair they were having and that was fine with him, but as he sat in his car outside of his parents' house, his mind couldn't help but replay the hurt look Renee had on her face as he stood there and accused her. *Did I have it all wrong?* He couldn't worry himself with thoughts of Renee at the moment. After storming out of Monica's house, he rushed over to his parents to finish what he should have with his father the day he saw him at his retirement party. They, all but Charles, had been calling him nonstop since that day. He had ignored their calls, but tonight he wanted to lay it all out in the open.

He stepped out of his car and could see thick streams of his breath in the air. It was cold outside to most given winter would make its arrival in Chicago in a few weeks, but the brutally windy night didn't phase Andrew. The fire of his anger was boiling high enough to cause a tea kettle to whistle on a stove top. He paused staring at the brown, brick, two-story house he had grown up in. He had so many fond memories of living there. He didn't know if he would get the same warm welcome he used to get when he stopped by for a visit, but again that didn't matter to him. He had questions he was determined to get answers to that night. Number one being, why did Charles rape Marie?

By the time he made it up to the house, the door swung open and his sister and mother, who had been peeking through the window watching him sit in his car, now stood in the doorway waiting for him to enter the house. Suddenly the courage and anger that propelled him to go to the house waned as he stared at his mother. He shook his head a little realizing he seemed to be disappointing all of the women in his life at that point. Maybe not all, he was still on Marie and Melanie's good sides.

He finally crossed the threshold and was unsure of how he would interact with his sister and mother. They both were cloaked with confusion and hurt.

Although she stood at the door until he entered the house, without speaking to him, his sister merely rocked her baby on her shoulder as she turned her nose up at Andrew and walked away from him. She made her way to the family room.

He still stood in the doorway staring at his mother. Every time she opened her mouth to speak, no words seemed to flow from it. She was only able to extend her hand out, directing him to the family room as she closed the door behind him.

He shoved his hands in his pockets as he walked the carpeted hallway to the family room. Being in the house humbled some of his anger until he saw Charles. His breathing sped up as he stared at him.

"Andrew, I see your chest heaving up and down. So I take it you're still mad for what you think I've done, but you will not disrespect me in my house." Charles grounded himself in place in case Andrew tried him again.

With his stare focused in on Charles, he made his way over to him. Elizabeth quickly made her way over to stand by her husband's side. So did Lisa. "I didn't step in when you attacked him at the party, but as your father said, you won't disrespect him, us, in our house. We're still your parents." Her voice trembled with the last of her statement. Lisa circled around them to comfort her mother as she began to cry.

Andrew turned his attention from his mother to continue his mission with his father. He came nose to nose with him. "You tell me not to disrespect you or your home, but don't you think it was absolutely disrespectful what you did to Marie?"

"I don't know what or who you're talking about." Charles walked away from Andrew and over to the French doors overlooking their spacious backyard. It was dark outside with nothing to stare at so he clearly saw Andrew's reflection as he walked towards him.

"So that day when I confronted you about it at the party, the look on your face let me know you knew who and what I was referring to, but now you're playing dumb?" Andrew raised his voice.

Elizabeth rushed over to stop Andrew's advancing steps toward Charles. "Watch your mouth, young man. Your father says he doesn't know what you're talking about and I believe him."

"Me, too." Lisa snarled as she worked to comfort her fussy baby.

Andrew laughed as he spoke. "I guess that's how I didn't believe it at first. You've had us all fooled all of these years. Had us thinking you were a good, loving man. You never let on that you were a rapist."

For the third time in months Andrew was slapped in the face by a woman.

"Watch your mouth. Do you hear me? Watch your mouth. I don't know who turned you against us, your father, but you straighten up now and stop with all of the lies and disrespect."

Andrew took a few steps back from his father and mother as he rubbed his jaw trying to calm the sting from the contact his mother's palm made with his face.

"You see what you've done? You have Mom thinking I've done something wrong when it's you. Why won't you just man up and tell the truth."

Charles said nothing, he simply lowered his head.

"Andrew, why don't you just go? Come back when you have some sense again," his sister called out to him.

"So you're not gonna man up? Tell the truth like you raised me to do?"

Charles remained silent and his body tensed more and more.

"Okay, since you won't tell it, I will." He looked to his mother and then to his sister before he spoke. "Remember how everybody used to joke that it must've been meant for me to be adopted into this family since I like so much like Charles?" Andrew couldn't even fix his mouth to call Charles his dad.

A faint smile covered Elizabeth's face as she remembered those many conversations and even having that thought the day they first saw him at the adoption agency.

"Well as twisted as a sense of fate would have it, I really am his son."

Elizabeth's eyebrows knitted together as she stepped closer to Andrew. "Of course you're his son, you're mine, too."

"No, Mom." Andrew rubbed her worried face. "He's my biological father."

She left Andrew's side and rushed to her husband's. "Charles, you've refused to say much about the matter since Andrew brought it up at the party. What is going on?"

"Yeah, *Dad,* tell her what you did and how I came to be." Andrew walked closer to his parents. So did Lisa as she cradled her sleeping baby.

"Charles, face me and tell me what's going on. I trust you, but we didn't raise Andrew to be a liar." The pitch and authority in her voice beckoned Charles to finally face them all.

His eyes were downtrodden and he stuffed his hands in his pocket as he stood there quiet.

"Charles! Say something." She now screamed in his face.

"It's obvious he's still as much of a coward as he was back then. Since he won't tell it, I'll continue." He looked into Elizabeth's eyes. "You know I reconnected with my birth mother because of my relationship with Melanie. Well, even though I was

249

and am enjoying building a relationship with her, you know I've always wanted to know my birth parents and their families."

She nodded her head with sadness visible in her eyes.

Andrew took note of her demeanor and redirected his thoughts. "You know it's not because I don't love you or appreciate what and who you've been to me, I just actually remember her, looking into her eyes. I needed to know her. Well after constantly asking her about my real dad, she finally let in that she had gotten raped and that's how she conceived me."

"I'm so sorry to hear that. So is that what's kept you away from us? Got you so worked up? But your father and I didn't have a hand in that."

Andrew laughed a maniacal laugh that had become his recent companion when around his dad. "That's the thing, he did."

Charles stepped back from them.

"She always said she would never tell who raped her, but after months of me badgering her and her actually seeing a picture of your husband, she admitted that Professor Dodson was the one who raped her in college."

Elizabeth stood completely still as what Andrew had told her filtered through her head. She inched her way closer to her husband until she stood directly in front of him.

His head was lowered. His chin touched his chest. He refused to look up at her. The always confident and authoritative Dr. Charles Dodson Sr. stood in front of her mute and timid.

"Charles," her voice was barely above a whisper, but those nearby could hear the fury brewing in her, "look me in my eyes and tell me what Andrew said is not true."

He never lifted his head and struggled to keep it down as she violently gripped his chin lifting his head so that his eyes could meet hers. "Tell me it's not true."

"I wish I could say it wasn't." He kept his voice low.

"What was that you said?" Andrew put his hand up to his ear and strained his neck towards Charles, egging him to speak up louder. "I don't think we heard you."

"It's true," he said loudly as he heaved a long, heavy sigh and rubbed his forehead. He brushed past them and walked over to the fireplace. He rested his elbows on the mantle and let his head fall into his hands.

"Dad!" Lisa's scream startled the baby and started her into a crying frenzy. Lisa was too shocked to tend to the baby just yet.

Elizabeth walked over to the wall where the light switch was and turned the lights on full bright. "Charles Dodson Sr., you tell me it isn't true what Andrew said you did? Tell me I didn't just hear you confess to raping his mother."

He remained quiet with his head low.

She rushed over to him and began pounding on his back. "Charles tell me it isn't true."

Andrew's smile started to fade. He thought his father's admission of raping Marie would set him free of the turmoil he had been going through since he found out the secret, but as he looked around the room at his distraught sister who looked like she would drop his niece at any moment, and then at his mother as she pounded on Charles's back and screamed, he realized he only meant for his father's admission to perhaps set him free. But it seemed to be doing more harm to his family than it was doing him any good. He walked over to his mother and pulled her away from his father.

"Charles, answer me." She pleaded with him as Andrew held her back.

Charles finally turned towards them. His eyes were red and glossy. "What am I supposed to say?

Would you all still look at me the same if I told you that yes I raped a woman when I was younger, before I met you." He stared into Elizabeth's eyes and tried to caress her face but she slapped his hand away from her.

"See that's why I never planned to tell any of you all that I raped a woman before and that Andrew was really my son, I knew you'd look at me differently."

"Wait, what?" Andrew released his mother and went to stand toe to toe with Charles. "You mean you knew you were my biological father?"

Charles hung his head. "Yes."

Elizabeth covered her mouth to quell her shriek. Lisa could see she was growing faint and ushered her mother to the nearby couch.

"What?" A knew surge of rage overtook Andrew and he shoved Charles forcefully causing him to fall back into the mantle.

"Ahhh." Charles bent over and gripped his back. He had hit the corner of it and the pain temporarily crippled him. No one reached out to help him or question how badly he was hurt. His wife and daughter just stared at him with a fresh look of confusion and hurt covering their faces.

Charles was still in so much pain that he let his body drop to the floor as he braced himself on his hands and knees. Andrew drew closer to him and hovered over him. "Get up and look me in my face and tell me everything. Why'd you rape her? How long have you known you were my real father?" Andrew spun in confusion as he huffed.

"I can't believe this shit." He turned back to Charles. "Get up and face me like a man."

Charles mustered up all of the strength he could and slowly rose from the floor as he braced his hand on his back. His face was now wet from the tears he had shed. When he made it eye level to his son, the rage he saw in Andrew's eyes honestly scared and pained him equally.

Andrew tightened his lips and clenched his fists as he spoke. "Answer my questions." His stare narrowed in on Charles demanding him to speak.

"I was a different man back then, so full of ambition. I had always managed to get what I wanted. I was where I wanted to be education wise and career wise too. I saw Marie and I wanted her, but she turned me down every chance she could. My obsession for her was so strong and like I said, I had gotten everything I wanted up to that point, so when I held her back in class that day and told her what I wanted from her but she didn't give it to me, I guess the narcissist in me snapped and I took it from her."

Andrew punched Charles right in the face causing him to fall back into the mantle yet again.

Lisa yelped but neither she nor her mother went to Charles's rescue.

Andrew stared at Charles as he said, "That's for taking what you wanted from her." His body was stiff and he was ready to unleash more of his rage on Charles as he walked towards him, but Charles threw his hands up in surrender.

"Enough, son, enough." Charles swallowed the blood in his mouth. He looked up at his son. "I'm sorry. I'm not that man anymore. After I did what I did, I realized I could never do it again. That wasn't the best version of a man I could be." He dropped his head and rubbed his swelling jaw.

Andrew snarled as he shook his head at Charles. "You are a sorry excuse for a man. When did you find out I was your son? And stand up and talk to me like a man." Andrew's voice elevated as he squared his shoulders and tightened his fists again.

"How can I stay on my feet when you keep knocking me off them?" Charles rose from the floor yet again. This time he headed over to the couch to sit next to his wife, but by the time his butt touched the seat of the couch, she jumped up from it and rushed across the room hugging herself tightly.

She couldn't bear to be next to him let alone look at him, but she just couldn't bring herself to leave the room. She, too, needed to hear what her husband had to say in response to Andrew's questions, especially him knowing he was Andrew's birth father.

Charles sat on the couch quietly and rested his head in his hands.

"I'm not done with you, answer my questions." Andrew walked over and smacked one of Charles's hands down from his face.

Charles slowly lifted his head and stared into Andrew's face. "You have every right to be angry and asking the questions you are, but if you put your hands on me one more time Andrew, I might have to kill you, or die trying." The authoritative stare in his eyes let Andrew know not to touch him anymore.

Still reeling with anger, Andrew backed up from Charles and sat on the arm of the couch across from him. He reasoned maybe the distance between the two of them would calm him some.

"Like you said, we always joked about how much you looked like me. I dismissed it until you brought home your school picture one year. I stared at it for a long time before I got all of my old school pictures and compared mine to yours. It was like looking at the same person in each. I dismissed the thought and years passed. Well you know, your mother always bathed you and whatnot when you were younger, but one day I walked in your room and you didn't have a shirt on. I saw you had the exact same Africa shaped birthmark I had on my right shoulder. Same location. Same size. Same color. I thought I was going crazy thinking you could possibly be mine, and I knew I hadn't cheated on my wife, but I remembered what I did to Marie, how old you were, and that it all could be true. Well, you had to go take your physical to start high school so I made sure I took you. I worked it out with the doctor to take a sample of your blood to compare to mine. Weeks later I found out that you actually were my biological son. It only made me love you more. I'm sorry, son." He looked up at Andrew hoping Andrew would know he really did love him. He then looked over to his wife. "I'm sorry, Liz, baby."

She stood up and walked over to him and stared him in the face. "I don't know you. You've had me living a lie all of this time." She walked out of the room and up to her bedroom crying.

Lisa cradled her baby as she shook her head speaking to her dad, "I don't know what to say. You were always my hero, but now..." She walked out of the room in search of her mother to comfort her.

Charles saw how disgusted his wife and daughter were with him, but since they had left the room, Andrew was the only one he felt he had hope of reconciling with at the moment. He stood from the couch moaning as the pains of being hit and pushed several times raked through his early sixty year old body. He took slow steps towards the man that really did look just like him physically, but nothing like him in character. He stayed an arm's length short of Andrew and decided to speak hoping to douse the fire burning in Andrew's eye. "I know what I did to Marie was wrong, but that's why I have been trying to make amends for my transgression against her by being the best father I could be to you, your brother, and your sister, the best husband to my wife, and just a good man all around."

"None of what you said could ever undo what you did," Andrew said through clenched teeth.

"I know it won't, but I'll never stop trying. Will you forgive me?" He looked into eyes shaped just like his pleading for forgiveness.

Andrew stood silent for a moment. It was apparent from the creases on his forehead and the downward curve of the corners of his mouth that he was contemplating what Charles asked him and yet still very much angry. He cleared his throat and looked Charles intently in his eyes. "No." He walked out of the house leaving Charles right in the middle of the family room.

21

Everyone stood in place frozen from the shock of Renee's admission. The newcomers in the room weren't all that phased and affected by Renee's statement. But judging from their gaping mouths, cocked heads, and wide eyes, the sisterhood and her brother, Keith, were still trying to digest what she'd just revealed.

Seeing that the women hadn't gathered their wits yet, Keith spoke up, "I'm sorry you all, we'll have to reschedule game night for another night. Thanks for coming, but I'm gonna have to ask you all to leave now."

"Of course, we understand," Vance said as he walked past Keith and shook up with him. The rest of his friends, brother, and sister-in-law followed behind him wishing them all a good night, except for Darius.

He made his way to Kim to see if she were alright. She looked as if every breath of air in her body had literally been knocked out of her. He put his arms around her and her body molded to his. She let the weight of what she had just been told by her triplet sister rest on his body, but his broad, strong, muscular frame supported her. "I'll call you before I come over tonight."

She said nothing. She simply nodded her head as he walked off and out the door.

Keith was on the ladies heels as Monica pulled Kim and Pam up the stairs with her. They all made it to the guest bedroom door believing Renee was in it, but when Monica sensed Keith was still behind them she spun around and faced him. "Where are you going?"

"In to talk to my sister. Find out about this son of hers she mentioned." Keith was about to knock on the door when Monica pulled him out of earshot of the door.

Pam supported Kim up with her body. She was still speechless. Gone was the feisty, in-your-face demeanor that always engulfed her. It had been replaced with hurt and bewilderment.

"Keith." Monica looker into her husband's eyes. "I know that's your triplet in there and that y'all share a special bond, but so do her and I. Obviously she was too embarrassed to tell any of us. Let us go in and try to get something out of her first. Then you can come in. Okay, babe?"

He turned his head away from her as if he were tuning her out, but she wrapped her arms around his waist, snuggled up closer to him, and planted kisses along his jawline.

He could never be mad at her long or resist her kisses. Just as she was going in for another kiss on his jaw, he turned to her and their lips met. It was a quick kiss, but with them, it was always heartfelt. "Okay. I'll give y'all ten minutes tops and if none of y'all come out by then, I'm coming in." He patted her on her ample butt as she walked away from him and back over to Pam and Kim.

He headed downstairs while they were still knocking on the door.

"Let us in." Monica stopped her knocking and pressed her ear to door

She heard nothing. She turned the knob and to all of their surprise, it wasn't locked. She led the pack into the room where they found Renee sprawled out across the bed weeping silently.

With what they had gone through with each other, and even within the last few years, Monica, Pam, and Kim knew that they had to walk the fine line of encouraging Renee to open up to them yet giving her the space and time to share her troubles of her own volition.

Luckily for them, Renee was tired of carrying her burden alone. She rolled over in the bed and sat up. Her face and eyes were puffy from crying so much and from gravity after being face down for so long. Monica rushed to the en suite bathroom to grab some tissue for Renee, while Kim and Pam quickly flanked her.

They didn't have to even bother asking her anything, she knew what they wanted to know after her shocking admission. Through her tears, she spoke as she attempted to pat her face dry of her nonstop tears. "Remember when we were at brunch about two years ago or so after Monica outed me for having an abortion just as she did?"

The looks on the others faces said that they recalled the brunch she was referring to. She continued with her story. "Well, I know I let you all believe that I'd actually had an abortion after Monica's slip of the tongue, but I just couldn't be honest with you all or myself at the time." Renee looked over at Kim's face that was wetter than hers. She could see that Kim was crushed. "Sissy." She grabbed Kim's hand and squeezed it. Kim didn't speak or move. "Sissy, I'm sorry. Say something. Do something. This is not like you to be so quiet."

Everyone's eyes were fixed on Kim awaiting her response.

Kim's five foot three frame jumped up from the bed, wiped her face, and fixed her stare on Renee. The others held their breath waiting for Kim's response to what was happening in the moment, she looked to be her old self.

"I'm still trying to digest what you just shared and since you haven't shared it all yet, I'm trying to keep my composure. But since you know me, you must know that I'm really hurt that as your sister, your triplet, you felt like you could never tell me that you gave birth to a baby and gave him up for adoption. You've been going through all of this on your own for years?" Kim took a deep breath. "And then there's another part of me that wants to slap you for not sharing any of it with me. I know we're all close, but I'm your sister." She choked on the last of her words as she stared into Renee's eyes. She saw the pain and remorse in Renee's eyes. She bent over and braced her hands on her knees. She let out a hushed wail as her back heaved up and down. It was the only way she knew how to respond amid all of the emotions circling her. Renee gathered herself from the bed and walked over to Kim. She rubbed her sister's back before she stood her up and the two women embraced one another. All Monica and Pam could hear were a repetition of "sorry, sorry, sorry" as the two sisters continued their emotional embrace. Moments later Renee loosened her hold on Kim and Kim took a seat on the gray, plush carpet near the bed and buried her chin in between her knees. Renee continued standing as she faced them. "Okay, I know you all have questions and I'll tell you soon, but right now, I'm so drained, I can't bear to speak any longer, let alone stand." Renee traipsed back over to the bed and fell on it face first. She immediately fell into a deep sleep, snoring and all.

The rest of the sisterhood stared at her incredulously and then at Keith as he busted through the door ready to hear Renee out.

He walked over to the bed confused. "What? Is she really asleep now?"

They each tried to shake her out of her slumber, but none of their attempts were successful.

22

The twins were with Keith's parents, leaving Monica and Keith with no one to attend to. That made it easier for them to camp out in the guest room where Renee had fallen asleep.

She woke up the next morning yawning and trying to adjust her eyes to the sunlight beaming through the window. When her eyes were fully adjusted, she wasn't surprised to see everyone up and alert staring at her. "Good morning," she said, yawning again.

"Good morning? Try good afternoon. We've all showered and ate breakfast while you just laid there like sleeping beauty, although we all know you aren't as pretty as me," Kim said, standing in front of Renee with her arms folded across her chest and tapping her foot. She was ready for the answers to her questions.

"Well I see the shock has worn off and you're back to your old crass self," Renee said as she stood up, trying to get past Kim, but Kim didn't budge. Renee finally gave in and flopped back down on the bed after a stare off with Kim.

"I sure am back to myself. You know, the one who gets answers by any means necessary."

Renee wrapped her arms tight around herself. "Stop staring at me. All of you."

"Sis, we aren't leaving this room, letting you leave it, or go back to sleep until we get some answers from you," Keith said.

"Okay, what do you wanna know?"

Kim stomped her foot and smacked her lips as her eyes bulged at Renee. "You have made me wanna hit you more times in these past couple of days than I ever had entire my life." With a dumbfounded look, she turned and stared at the others. "She has the nerve to ask us what we wanna know!" She turned back to Renee before continuing. "What we want to know is how and why you chose to give birth to a whole human being on your own, give him up for adoption and not tell us about it? Did Ted make you do it?" She pointed her finger at Renee.

"Not at first." She lowered her head and barely audible, she continued to speak. "But he's the reason why I did it."

The fire had left Kim just that quick. She sat down next to Renee and squeezed her, clinging on to her waist. "I'm sorry, sissy, that that jerk treated you the way he did and made you feel like you couldn't come to us. I just don't get why you've kept it all a secret from us."

Monica spoke up. "Renee, I know that you've clearly dealt with a lot on your own, but why'd you make me think you had got an abortion like I did? You made me feel like you understood me." Monica's hazel eyes were glossy.

Renee stood up and swiped her face of the tears that had stained it. Her normally calm and reserved demeanor would have to take a backseat in order to answer all of their questions and perhaps allay her feelings. "Monica, I'm sorry, but the only reason I made up the whole story about me getting an abortion was because you spotted me at the clinic. I had learned days before that I was too far along to abort, so I was there to see a worker about the adoption procedure. Getting an abortion was the only thing I could think to tell you to explain why I was there. You and I both know that particular section of the clinic was only about preventative measures for pregnancy. And trust me when I say that while I now know that my son is still alive, but your child isn't, not a day goes by where I don't feel bad for what I did. The child may not have died, but a big part of my spirit did when I gave him up."

With tears streaking her rich mocha face, Monica just stared at Renee. Keith went over to her and rubbed her shoulders.

Renee knew she had to make up her big lie to Monica somehow, too.

"But, sissy, why'd you think you couldn't talk to us?" Kim called out clutching a pillow. Keith then went over to his sister and rubbed her back and she began to cry silently.

"I'm sorry, Kim, but I couldn't keep the baby around Ted. I was afraid he might harm the baby. Do you know that fool told me that I couldn't have the baby because then the baby would take my attention away from him?" She asked no one in particular. "He wanted the focus on no one but him."

Keith's nostrils flared and his fists balled up. "I wish you all would have let me handle him back then the way I wanted to. You wouldn't have had to deal with any of his mess let alone give your baby up for adoption."

"We know, Keith, but we didn't want you to risk your future on that jerk." Kim patted her brother's knee.

Renee continued. "He told me that I had to get an abortion, but I kept delaying it until I was too far along to terminate. I kept myself away from you all because of the abuse, so hiding the pregnancy from you all wasn't an issue for me."

"Well how did you manage to hide it from him if you were living with him? He never let us in you all's apartment and our class schedules never coincided at all that year. The few times we worked our schedules to camp outside of your class to see you when you came out, he would appear out of nowhere and rush you away from us. You never fought to be around us or let us in your life that year." Kim took a deep breath trying to keep her hurt and angry emotions at bay.

"I know I was wrong, sissy, but my head was in a different place then. I wasn't always assure of myself like you were. He came in and preyed on that. I fell under his spell until I woke up from it. And I was able to keep the pregnancy from him because I carried the baby in my breasts, butt, and hips. He liked the way I had filled out. In fact, he was groping me and trying to have sex with me when I went into labor."

Pam's heart shaped and Monica's oval shaped faces both contorted in anger as Kim jumped up and paced the floor in frustration.

"Where is he now? I'll still kill him," Keith chimed in.

"I'll share that in a second. Let's let Renee continue with her story." Kim finished her statement as eyes of wonder locked in on her. "What? Y'all know me. Keep going, Renee."

Renee shook her head questionably at Kim, but continued her story. "He thought I was moaning in anticipation of what he wanted to do with me, but I guess once my water broke and he felt the gush of fluid on his hand, then hit the floor, he stepped back from me with his eyes wide. 'What was that?' he asked. I held my breath as I watched the moment sink into his brain. The minute I saw the embers of fire fully lit in his eyes, I tried to make a run for it, but my contractions had gotten the best of me at that point and instead of running, my knees buckled under me as I fell to the floor in pain."

Kim shrieked and covered her mouth.

Renee continued through her tears and choked some on her words. "He beat me real bad then took me to the hospital. Of course, everyone was staring at my fresh cuts and bruises while I delivered the baby. After I delivered, the nurse came in and asked what we wanted to name the baby. Ted immediately spoke up saying it didn't matter because we were going to give the baby up for adoption. He didn't even know that I had already chosen to do that, but the nurse left immediately for whatever reason. Thank you, God." She mumbled the last of her words to herself. She shivered subtly as she cried. Kim went to her side and held her. "I could see it in the nurse's eyes that she was wary of the two of us. She came back in with a folder saying that she saw in it that I had already taken the necessary steps to secure an adoption for the baby and that Ted needed to sign the papers giving away his parental rights. He looked over at me and told me that I had better already had that taken care of since I didn't get the abortion like he told me to. He snatched the papers from her and signed wherever the 'x's' indicated him to. Well after he signed his name for the last time, the nurse walked to the door and signaled someone to come in."

"Who?" Kim asked in anticipation.

"Let her finish," Monica scolded Kim.

"You four trip me out," Keith said as he shook his head in astonishment of the women's banter at the moment.

"It was a police officer. The nurse had called him."

"Yes!" Kim pumped her fist in the air.

"Well, I wasn't so sure of what would happen when the officer came in. Even though he'd been by my side the whole time, Ted thought I had called the police on him. He lunged at me and barely had his hands around my neck when the officer grabbed him and restrained him. Of course he was resisting, but he was no match for the officer. He calmed in the officers arms and started laughing saying that the officer had to let him go because I would never press charges against him anyway.

"The officer informed him that even if that were true, there was enough evidence on my body to prove otherwise, not to mention he would be charged with attempted murder on the child since he beat me while I was in labor. The nurse chimed in saying that with the severity of my bruises and swelling she could clearly see the intent to kill me and the child. Ted became irate again screaming that the charges would never stick as long as I didn't file charges against him.

"I was a mess and in pain. I was hurt over giving up my baby, sad that I didn't have you all there with me, even though I know that was my fault. I was quiet for a long time as the officer used his strength to subdue Ted. The nurse came to my side and squeezed my hand and told me not to be afraid of Ted. She said I needed to be strong and charge him so that it won't happen again to me or any other woman for that matter. She whispered a scripture in my ear that pierced my core and reminded that I was a child of God and that I should fear no evil. My mouth flew open letting the officer know that I would indeed press charges against Ted. He dragged Ted out of there kicking and screaming. The nurse said that the police told her when she called that even if I didn't press charges, the prosecutor could charge him."

"So when did you contact us in all of this?" Kim asked clearly still in shock from the wideness of her already big, round eyes.

Renee lowered her head, averting eye contact with any of them. "A couple of days after I gave birth. I wanted my body to heal some after just having a baby and being beaten so badly. I would've waited until the swelling went down and the bruises fully went away, but I just felt so alone, I needed y'all around."

"Well I'm glad you called us at all." Kim hugged Renee.

"Kim, I can't breathe. You're squeezing me too tight."

"So what. This is for all of that love that you apparently felt you were missing that made you think you had to accept what that jerk did to you."

Pam interrupted their love fest. "You can be insensitive at times, Kim."

"Whatever," Kim said.

Pam ignored her. "And Renee, not that I care about him, but what happened with Ted? Did you have to go to court to see the charges through?"

"No, I thought I would have had to, but I received a letter saying I didn't need to. It said he had plead to a deal. I verified through the state's prison database as well."

"And that part was in thanks to me." Kim grinned as she pointed to herself.

"What?" Renee's face scrunched up as she stared at Kim.

The others sat on the edge of their seats but only Keith spoke up. "You mean you knew all of that had went on and didn't tell us either?"

"Of course I didn't know about the baby, but after I saw the way my sister looked when she finally called us, I did some digging to find out where he was. I was happy to know that he was in jail, but because Renee was so tight lipped with what had gone on between them, I wasn't sure how long he'd actually be in there, so I went to visit him."

Keith shook his head at his fearless sister, Kim.

Renee seemed to hold her breath as she stared at Kim before speaking, "I can't believe you. What happened when you saw him?"

Kim stood up from the bed and unlocked her arm from Renee's. She stood in the middle of the room and began her theatrical retelling of the day she went to see Ted in jail. "You know I've always worn heels, no matter where I go, I like the way they perk my butt up—"

"Kim!" They all managed to shout her name at the same time.

"Okay, okay, okay, I'll get back to the story. I brought up my always wearing heels to say that I didn't wear them that day. I wore my gym shoes just in case I had to throw down with him. I didn't know if there would be glass between us to protect him from me or if the guards would restrain him if need be if we'd both be out in the open. There was glass between us, luckily for him. I didn't even sit down on the little dingy stool they had there. I stood and looked him straight in the eyes as I talked through the receiver and told him that if he ever tried to contact Renee again that I would personally cut his stuff off and shove it down his throat."

Keith winced as he clinched his knees together. The rest of the sisterhood shook their heads knowing that Kim was crazy enough to do what she threatened if given the chance.

She stared at them matter-of-factly and continued speaking, "Yup, I sure did tell him that. Told him that if he didn't take a deal or something that would keep my sister from having to testify against him in court and having to relive the hell he put her through, what I told him I would do to him earlier was child's play compared to what I would do to him."

"He always did think you were crazy," Renee said. "That's why he didn't want me to be around you. He said I was sweet and innocent. Said he didn't know how you hadn't rubbed off on me up to that point, but he couldn't trust me changing into you if I didn't stay away from you."

Kim shook her head battling a mixture of emotions and questions as she looked at Renee. She dismissed them and continued on with her story. "I was ready to leave after I said my piece to him, but he started to speak as I was almost at the door causing me to go back and hear what he had to say just out of curiosity. You would not believe that worthless nigga said that while he loved Renee and didn't want her with anyone else, he didn't want to and couldn't handle being in jail. He said with the time he was facing, he couldn't afford to deal with Renee anymore. I told him I was glad he felt the same way I did. He waited until I turned my back and was walking away from him again before he blurted out, 'Besides, Renee's weak anyway. When I get from up under this, I'm gonna find me a strong woman that can handle me.' I flipped him the bird and asked the guard to let me out as I heard him calling me all kinds of names and saying something he bet I didn't know."

"I swear, you've always been a mess." Monica chuckled and shook her head causing her ebony, wavy, shoulder length hair to brush back and forth across her shoulders like the bristles of the brush at a carwash do on the headlights of a car running through it.

"Yup, especially when it comes to my baby sister and brother." She squeezed both Renee and Keith's cheeks.

Keith pulled away from her and turned his attention back to Renee. "I don't get it, sis. You've never really talked to me about it, so I just don't get why you felt like you had no other options but to be with someone like him."

Kim stepped in to answer for Renee. "You know she's always been that naive church girl. She attracted the bad boys in high school and she dismissed them all, but Ted's old dirty—"

Renee held her hand to silence the expletives she knew were sure to come from Kim's mouth. She could see just how heated Kim was talking about Ted and decided to answer Keith's question for herself. "Kim's kind of right, almost. Bad boys have never been my type and Ted didn't present himself like that at first. He was kind and thoughtful at first. It wasn't until after I had fallen hard for him and had sex with him," she turned her head from her brother but continuing, "that he started changing on me."

Keith smiled as he tilted Renee's face back towards him. "It's okay, Renee. I knew you two," he pointed at Kim and Renee, "would have sex at some point. Shoot I couldn't wait to have sex with Monica." He turned and winked at Monica.

Pam gave him a scolding look.

"What? I meant after we got married. Right, Monica?" He looked to Monica to come to his rescue.

"Yes. Leave my baby alone. He was a gentleman with me. He waited until we got married before he had me whichever way he wanted. How do you think the twins came to be?" she said to no one in particular as she blew a kiss to Keith.

Kim pretended to gag. "Would you two stop it? The spotlight should still be on Renee." Kim held her hand up over Renee as if shedding a flashlight on her.

Renee ignored Kim and continued to speak as she looked to her brother. "Like I told them, he was my first and I wanted him to be my only, so I felt if I prayed for him, for us, maybe he'd change. That's why I stayed with him through the abuse."

"I hope you all know now that you can't change a man. He has to want to change on his own. You can't be his savior. If he's not already in position to be the man you want and need him to be when you meet him, then he either ain't the one, or it ain't the right time for y'all. Just keep doing what you're supposed to do and God will send the right one at the right time."

"Yes, He will," Monica said, smiling as she made her way over to Keith and planted a wet kiss on his lips before she took a seat on his lap.

He held her around her waist as he smiled at her. "Yes, He will."

Kim snarled at them as she shifted her attention to Renee. "Okay so we got the Ted part out of the way, but what about my nephew? Did Marcus track him down? Is he alright? Do you plan to get him back? He belongs in our family, you gotta get him back." Kim was so frantic and jittery as she sounded off her questions to Renee.

Fresh tears glowed in Renee's deep, brown eyes. "Yes, Marcus found him. He's just as handsome as he can be. In fact he looks just like Keith. He looks healthy and we'll adjusted, but I only saw a few pictures of him."

"Okay, so when are we going to get him back?" Kim asked.

"I don't know if I can."

Kim rushed to Renee's side and began to rub her back as she slumped over crying.

23

Andrew hadn't talked to anyone in the past two weeks. The only people he had been accepting calls from where Melanie and Marie, and even then he was short with them and asked that they give him time to sort through everything he had learned. They respected his wishes, although Marie still called him every day just to say hi and let him know that she was there for him any time of the day. But other than them, he only interacted with his clients and those he made deals with for his clients.

He sat on his couch reading the specifics of a contract while Karen's sports broadcast played in the background. Hearing her recap a game the way she was brought a faint smile to his face. He hadn't worn one in a long time, but hearing her voice made him think about how lucky Kyle was to find the love of his life. He hoped he could share the same joy with a women in time. Although now that he knew the truth of how he came to be and who his birth parents were, he realized that it still didn't fulfill him the way he thought it would.

He dropped the papers on the side of him and relaxed on the couch. He thought that the only time he felt fulfilled was when he was either praying with Renee or down at Marcus' church interacting with the men's ministry. And just like that his phone rang. It was Marcus. He'd been ignoring his calls as well, but trying to find some peace within himself and begin to get past all that he'd been through, he answered his phone. "Hello."

"Hello. I wasn't sure you'd answer the phone given how many times I've called with no answer from you."

Andrew remained silent.

"It's cool though, I can only imagine what you're going through with what you told me at first."

"You don't know the half of it." Andrew rubbed his face.

"I don't, but I do want you to know, as I've said on the voicemails, you had it all wrong about me and Renee."

"Yeah, I got your voicemails. I believe you."

"Whew. I'm glad you know that I'm one of the brothas out here that really does love his wife and is sold out for God. I ain't saying I'm perfect, but adultery? No sir, not me."

Andrew laughed a little. "I got you. So what were you helping Renee with?"

"I can't share that with you. I won't betray her confidence, but I take it that you haven't talked to her yet?"

"I can understand you keeping her secret and no I haven't talked to her since that night." Andrew sat up and shook his head before he let it drop into his hand. "I doubt if she'll ever talk to me again after how I talked to her and what I accused her of."

"I don't know about her never talking to you again, but what she is dealing with ain't a secret anymore."

"Hunh?"

"Well after you left, all eyes were on her and me. I couldn't let my wife think that I had broken our vows, but I didn't want to be the one to out Renee."

Andrew scratched his head wondering what Renee was hiding.

Marcus continued. "So she blurted out what I had been helping her do."

There was silence.

"Andrew, you still there?"

"Yeah."

"So what are you gonna do?"

282

"About what?"

"Renee."

"Nothing. What is there for me to do?"

"I could tell from the way you talked about her, even though I didn't know who you were talking about when you always managed to bring her up in our conversations, that you really liked her. You valued her and whatever was going on between y'all."

Andrew fell back on the couch and nodded his head as if Marcus could see him.

"Andrew, you still there?"

"Yeah. Just thinking. I mean I'm still in the dark about her secret so I don't know what to think, and like I said, why would she even forgive me after how I talked to her that night?"

"I hear ya and I understand that you were dealing with some heavy stuff, but so is Renee, and for all of the time she prayed for and comforted you the way you said she did, she just may need that back from you now."

"So you've talked to her?"

"Yeah, she came by to apologize to me and my wife for the confusion. I already knew what she was dealing with and I could see that it was still heavy on her. My wife and I prayed for her, but if y'all really had become as close as you said you two had become, you probably would be of more comfort to her than anyone else right now."

"And how can you be so sure of that? Holy Spirit told you that?" Through Marcus and Renee, Andrew had come to better understand the roles that each member of the Trinity played. He had learned that the Holy Spirit gives insight.

Marcus laughed. "If you wanna say that, then yes."

"Okay, but man has free will, right?"

"Yup."

"So Renee might use her free will to ignore me forever."

"That could be true, but I doubt it."

"I don't know, and besides I still need to figure out my family thing."

"Okay yes, you should be ready emotionally and spiritually before you pursue her. I don't know what else happened with you and your fam in these past two weeks, but don't be afraid to step out on faith and trust that things could actually turn out in your favor where Renee is concerned. Sometimes we try and wait until we have everything together in our lives before we make the next move, but sometimes we won't make the next best move until we step out on faith like I said."

"Okay, I'll think about that, and thanks for not holding a grudge against me."

"No problem. Only a man who has sincere feelings for a woman would overreact the way you did." Marcus laughed.

"I don't know about all of that." Andrew smirked.

"Well, I do. I gotta get going, but remember that you can always hit me up when you need to talk or pray. And I hope that you make it back down to the church on a Wednesday night soon."

"Yeah, I need to." Andrew exhaled a deep sigh.

"Say, Andrew?"

"Yeah, man."

"Have you accepted Christ as your Lord and Savior?"

Andrew pondered the question long and thoughtfully before he finally responded to Marcus. "Yeah, I grew up in church."

"Naw, I mean, have you allowed God into your heart to the point where you not only accept Christ's finished work on the cross, which means you let Him be your savior, but equally important, have you, are you, willing to allow Him to guard your heart and guide your steps? Mold you into a better man as your Lord?"

Andrew rubbed his forehead as he contemplated the weight of Marcus's question. "Yeah, I'm tired of living the way I am. Doing things my way hasn't gotten me any closer to who I want to be and what I want to have."

"Okay, just repeat this prayer after me. Continue to pray and let Him in your heart more and more and keep coming to church to get fed the Word to strengthen you. That's how He becomes your Lord. Okay, now repeat after me, Heavenly Father—"

Andrew sat up completely erect and repeated Marcus's words aloud.

Marcus continued, "I come to You in the Name of Your Son Jesus Christ—"

Andrew repeated him yet again.

"You said in Your Word, according to Romans ten and thirteen that whosoever shall call upon the name of Your Son Jesus shall be saved…by faith I now confess Jesus Christ as my new Lord and from this day forward, I dedicate my life to serving Him." Marcus finalized his portion of the prayer.

"…I dedicated my life to serving Him." Andrew repeating the last of Marcus's words and smiled the brevity of what he'd done. "I didn't feel the earth move like I thought it would. Am I done?"

Marcus laughed. "Everyone doesn't experience an 'otherwordly' moment as some people would like to believe. Your conversion has occurred. You confessed Him, so you belong to Him, but yes, your journey is just beginning with learning how to live for Him. It's a daily process, but possible and worth it with God as your Lord. Like I said, just pray, read the word daily to strengthen your spiritual muscles and you'll be alright."

"Thanks," Andrew said.

"No problem. Take care," Marcus said.

"Aiight. You, too." Andrew ended the call.

Andrew kept his phone in his hand and rested his other forearm on his forehead as he stared across the room at nothing at all. He was glad he'd made a step to get closer to God. His mind drifted to Renee. *I wonder if she'll answer the phone if I call her.* He decided he would take Marcus's advice and reach out to Renee. He still didn't know how he would move forward with his mom and dad, but he knew that he wanted, needed, Renee in his life. It was time to make amends with her and see how she was doing. He pressed the button making his screen active again and pressed the one button he needed to on his keypad to speed dial her. He put the phone on speaker as it began to ring. It was the evening time, so he knew she should be available to talk. If she kept the same schedule she had before, she wasn't at church at the moment. He stared at the seconds on the clock change into minutes with still no answer. Her voicemail prompted him to leave a message. He sat up and wiped his face, preparing himself to speak. "Renee…"

24

Andrew didn't know what to do with himself. He was thriving with the deals he was making for his clients. He was back to attending the men's ministry meetings, and while he knew it may not have been the most mature thing for him to do, he had settled into a comfortable habit of ignoring all of the Dodson's calls. But there was just one thing that kept him uneasy throughout his day, the fact that he hadn't talked to Renee in over a month. He left her that voicemail after Marcus first called him after his blowup at Monica's house, but since that one call, he couldn't gather the courage to let her phone ring long enough for her voicemail to kick in. The minute his phone registered that he was calling her, he would end the call. He sat on his couch and shook his head, acknowledging the fact that he did that at least three times a day. He missed her sweet voice, her prayers, the way she tried to hide her smile when she was around him. Their late night phone conversations. There was so much to her that he missed. And he definitely wanted to talk to her about growing closer to God day by day.

He found himself setting aside time in the morning to talk to God and meditate on the scripture his online bible calendar sent him. *So why haven't I called her then?* It was nine a.m. on a chilly Tuesday morning and he didn't have any meetings scheduled for the day. He didn't have to fly out for business until the next night, and he knew he didn't want to leave for his weeklong trip without explaining himself to her and hopefully her opening up to him. He knew the latter would be a long stretch after the way he behaved, but his newly discovered courage where Renee was concerned egged him on to give it a shot.

His newfound resolve of setting things straight with her made him jump off the couch and scurry to his master bath to get ready to see her. He was piecing his plan together as he sailed around his ship themed bathroom, but he knew that by the time he left his house, stopped to pick up flowers, get her favorite foods from their coffee shop, and get to the side of town where she worked, he would be right on time for what he remembered was the time she normally took her lunch.

He couldn't wait to see her, he just hoped she would somehow feel the same.

***

Renee had finally decided to go to lunch with her coworkers. Her time with them was much needed. Knowing how often she had went to the hospital to sit with Brandon and pray for him, they tried to comfort her from the news earlier that week that her superiors decided to pull the plug on him. While she hated that his short life ended the way it did, she didn't blame God for Him not healing Brandon on this side. She was mature enough in Christ to know that while the pain of losing a loved one was real, a person's prayers for God to heal that sick person sometimes ended up with them receiving their healing in heaven, where there is absolutely no sickness or diseases.

While she knew she might mourn Brandon for quite some time, the few coworkers she dined with for lunch helped her to rejoice with the news that Phillip had been placed with a family who had started the process to adopt him. What occurred with the boys had reminded her that there was a time and a season for everything. While Brandon's outcome may not have looked right for others, she knew that God does all things well and Phillip's well-being was definitely being cared for by his new family.

Temporarily relieving her emotions of Brandon and Phillip, she actually enjoyed herself, and her time with them helped to escape her thoughts of whether or not she would try to be a part of her son's life. She didn't want to upset the life that he knew, but she honestly wanted to be a part of his. The added pressure from her brother, sister, and parents to make him apart of their family and bring him where they thought he belonged didn't help her dismiss the thought of leaving him be at all. One thing she had become grateful for was that those closest to her knew her secret. In those moments where she really felt bad about what she did, she would call one of them and they would pray for her and encourage her not to beat herself up. They reminded her that God had forgiven her and he would make all things new in her life. She believed that and she was working to trust Him more and more day by day, to make good on His promise of giving her peace that would surpass all understanding of the situation.

Most importantly, she was learning to forgive herself. The ongoing updates that Marcus had given her about her son comforted her in that she no longer wondered if the beating she suffered while giving birth to him had done any cognitive damage to him, it hadn't. He was a straight A student and turning out to be an all American athlete like his Uncle Keith. She found out that he was on the varsity community football team even though his twelve years of age warranted him to be in the junior league. And no longer did she have to worry if he had been mistreated by his adoptive parents. Marcus didn't discover any medical mishaps for him that couldn't be tied to a sporting event. With that knowledge she was able to relax more.

It wasn't until she made it to her floor at work that she begin to feel something she hadn't felt in a while, an awareness of someone's presence. She didn't know who, but as she made it closer to her office door, a faint yet intoxicating scent filled her nose and she immediately smiled remembering that Andrew wore a cologne similar to it. The closer she got to her office, the stronger the scent became and she knew it was his distinct smell. But because she couldn't see past the tops of the cubicles, she didn't know if someone was indeed sitting in the chair outside her door. She tried to dismiss thoughts of him, but the smell reminded her of time spent with him. She hadn't talked to him since that night he blew up at her. Although she thought it was wrong what he did, looking back, she guess she could see how her being stealth with Marcus could make someone question their actions. And even though Kim was still mad at him for how he hollered at her, she had pointed out to her that only a man who cared about a woman would feel so betrayed by the thought of her being with someone he was cool with. She didn't necessarily doubt that that was his case, but that was neither here nor there for her. She would just work through missing him like crazy until the feelings she had for him completely vanished.

She sighed, hoping they would end soon as she rounded the last cubicle before she made it to her door. Shock gripped her body and caused her to still her steps as she stared at the source of the intoxicating scent sitting in the chair outside of her office door. He saw her and stood with his hands loaded. He had a dozen orchids in one hand and a dark woven picnic basket in the other. The smile he wore held a certain uncertainty. She struggled to find the words to say as she inched closer to her door, ultimately inching closer to him.

She stopped a foot short of him. "Drew, what are you doing here?" She unconsciously began smoothing her hair down and adjusting her clothes.

He smiled at her movements. *She is still so beautiful when she's nervous.* "Hoping that I could speak with you." He raised one eyebrow with his lips pressed together with hope.

She looked around to see if anyone saw him standing in front of her with the picnic basket and flowers in his hands. She couldn't tell if they had, but she rushed him into her office before anyone got wind of him being there for her. She knew Amina would tease her and never let her hear the end of a man coming to see her at work.

Once she felt she was safe in her office with the door locked behind her, she took a deep breath and wiped the sweat beads on her forehead. She looked up to see him staring at her and gave him a half smile as she began to clear space on her desk for the flowers.

He tried to quell his laughter as he stared at her dropping things as she cleared her desk and a chair, all the while trying to avoid eye contact with him.

She was finally done and barely looked at him as she stretched her hand out, suggesting he sit in the chair in front of her desk.

He sat and held onto the flowers as he sat the basket in the space she had cleared on her desk. He stared at the rest of her office, taking in all of the books she had in relation to being a social worker. He could tell from the mounds of folders sprawled around her office really had seen a lot kids with varying backgrounds given as many files as there were. When she finally sat down, he couldn't see her face because the basket blocked his view of her. She didn't bother to move it.

He laughed as he removed the basket from the desk, but the weight of the bouquet reminded him he was still holding them and hadn't yet given them to her. He got up from his seat and rounded her desk until he stood next to her. "Renee?"

She refused to look up at him, so he squatted to be eye level with her. "Renee?"

Feeling like she had no choice, she finally turned to look at him. When she did, she locked eyes with him and they gazed into each other's eyes for what seemed like hours before he decided to break the peaceful yet intense silence between them.

"Here, these are for you." He placed the bouquet in her arms.

"Thank you. They're beautiful. Let me go put them in water." She swiveled in her seat and tried to lift from her chair but he kept both his hands on her knees causing her to remain seated. His touch alarmed her. Her body trembled, but she hoped he didn't know it. The reserved look on his face led her to believe he didn't know the affect his closeness was having on her, and she managed to relax some. Her eyes focused on his hands still on her knees while his eyes was focused on her.

When he realized where her eyes were fixated, he removed his hands from her knees. "I'm sorry, I just didn't want you to run out of here or something." She opened her mouth to speak but he spoke up first. "I owe you so many apologies, but let me first start off by apologizing for showing up here today unannounced. I leave town tomorrow and I just couldn't let another day pass, let alone a week, without seeing you, talking to you, explaining my crazy behavior at game night."

Renee cleared her throat as she rubbed the back of her neck. Her body tensed as he reminded her of that night.

He could see her shifting in her seat and knew he needed to keep talking to keep her from retreating in herself the way he knew she could. "Renee, I had to come here today, look you in the face, and apologize from the bottom of my heart for being the jerk I was that night." He stood up and stretched his legs out but he remained close to her. Him standing up forced her to look up at him. "I know I should've apologized to you sooner than now, but I didn't know if you would even be willing to hear me out, especially since you didn't answer my call. I was wrong. I had no business calling you out like that. You and I weren't a couple. It honestly wasn't my business if you were creeping with Marcus or not."

Renee jumped up out of her seat and in his face.

He put her arms back down to her sides knowing what she was about to say to him. He laughed.

Her eyebrows knitted together and she frowned as she said, "What's so funny?" She tried to pull away from him, but he held a gentle yet firm grip on her wrists.

"I can't help it. It just took a lot out of me not to kiss you when you jumped in my face. It's something I've been wanting to do."

She pulled away from him again and he knew he needed to let her go this time. He could see how flustered and embarrassed she was at his admission.

She turned completely away from him and fanned herself.

"Relax. I won't try to kiss you now. I still owe you so many more apologies, plus there is some stuff we need to lay all out on the table before we discuss *us*."

"Us?" She turned to face him with a small amount of excitement in her voice, but it was overpowered by the confused look on her face.

"Yes, an *us*, but like I said, that's not the topic of discussion now. Let me get back to apologizing to you, woman. Please have a seat again." He smiled as he rounded the desk again and they both retook their seats at the same time. "You didn't let me finish.

Although you and Marcus were your business, I know now it wasn't the way I thought it was."

Her shoulders relaxed.

"I just felt so betrayed by my dad at the time because of what I had learned that when I saw you with Marcus more than once, I jumped to the wrong conclusion. The two people who I thought was there for me at the time, were being foul. My assumption does not excuse my behavior that night, especially for the way I talked to and treated you, but I'm just telling you that's where my head was at the time."

She said nothing as she looked down at her hands twiddling in her lap.

He wasn't sure if she was still too nervous to look directly at him or if she just didn't care what he was saying.

He knew he needed to bare it all in hopes that she would better understand him and perhaps his outburst with her that day. He scooted to the edge of his chair and rested his forearms on her desk. "I know that I never really told you all about my frustration with my adoption." He lowered his head for a moment and rubbed his face.

Renee took note of his demeanor and she relaxed in her chair. She could tell that what he was sharing with her was the source of all that pain she always saw in his eyes. She hoped he'd share it all with her, released it all, and that he would find peace in his situation sooner than she would in hers.

He finally lifted his head. He locked eyes with her and he could see her pleading with him to continue, so he did. "Of course, I've always wanted to know my birth parents since I was a little boy and even when I met Marie, my birth mom, the desire to know my birth father was still strong. Despite knowing that the man raped her, I still wanted to know who he was." He stood and paced the floor. "I pleaded with Marie to tell me who he was until one day she finally did."

Renee held her breath not knowing where Andrew's story would turn.

He stopped pacing the floor and looked to her. "You will not believe who she told me my father was."

Renee was almost afraid to ask but she sensed that her participation in the conversation would comfort him into continuing. "Who?"

"She told me that my father, Charles Dodson Sr., the man who raised me, was my birth father." Andrew gripped the back of the chair he once sat in. He was trying to subdue the anger bubbling in him. He was there to apologize to Renee for his erratic behavior. He couldn't afford to have another meltdown in front of her. He leaned completely over the chair and took deep breaths to further calm himself down when he felt the gentle caress of Renee's hand spanning his back.

"Andrew, calm down. Have a seat."

Her desire to comfort him made him emotional and he sniffed the tears that were threatening to make their appearance on his face. He stood up with his back towards her and composed himself, taking subtle, deep breaths before he finally turned to face her again. And when he did, he got lost in that angelic face of hers. She gave him a calming smile before she walked back to her seat at her desk.

He followed suit and returned to his. "I'm sorry. I'm trying to keep it together in front of you. I don't want you to think I'm a mad man that can't control my emotions. It's just that I feel like I've been living a lie my whole life. The man I grew up admiring and wanting to be like turns out to be a monster."

Renee didn't know what to say. Every time she opened her mouth to speak nothing came to her to help him make sense of what he had found out about his dad.

He didn't know what was going through her head that made her open and close her mouth without speaking, but he didn't want any more assuming and certainly not any secrets between them, so he decided to continue to plead his case with her. "Again, I'm not trying to excuse my behavior that night, but knowing the truth about my dad and then to think that the woman I had grown so fond of wasn't being honest with me either, I just snapped."

Renee was silent for what seemed like light years to him. He spoke up again. "Say something, will you? Please?"

"I don't know what to say. That's a lot you were, are, dealing with. Although I definitely don't agree with how you handled yourself with me, I know what it's like for everything bottled inside of you to just spill over one day." She let her words linger in the air causing Andrew to stare at her with an uncertain curiosity.

"I know I have so much more making up to do with you, but do you forgive me?" He put his hands up in a praying motion and tried to give her his best impression of sad puppy dog like eyes.

She smiled a little. "God soften your heart? You have control over that and you're right, you have a lot of making up to do, but I'll forgive you. I've done a lot I've had to be forgiven for." She wrung her hands together under the desk and began to avert eye contact with him again.

"Renee?"

"Yes." She refused to look up at him.

"Although my recent behavior may not lead you to think so, but you know you can trust me, right?"

"I guess." She slowly lifted her head up at him.

"We both kept something big from one another. I've shared mine, will you share yours with me?"

She could barely be heard when she spoke, "I'm afraid to. You may not look at me the way you do now after you find out what I did."

He reached across her desk and beckoned for her to place her hands in his.

She surprisingly acquiesced him.

Tears streamed her face as she began to speak. Not so much that she was still reeling in what she had done years back, but from the uncertainty of how Andrew would react once he knew it all. She freed one of her hands from his and wiped her face. She placed it back in his as he beckoned for her to do so and warily looked him in his eyes as she said, "You wanted me to accept your apology and the story that caused it, you should be willing to accept what I have to tell you."

"I will."

"I was in an abusive relationship in undergrad that led to me getting pregnant and ultimately giving up the baby for adoption, although I led my sister and best friends to believe that I actually had an abortion. I've carried the guilt of giving my baby up for adoption all of these years. It's eaten at me so much as I've looked through case after case of children being taken from abusive homes and often times being placed in abusive homes. It's made me wonder if my son was suffering the same fate that many of the kids I rescued had suffered. That guilt motivated me to do the best I could in placing each kid in the best home possible. I didn't know if you would even like me anymore, if even only as a friend, if I shared with you the fact that I had given a child up for adoption seeing as though you had been as well and it had been a sore spot for you all of your life."

"Renee, I would never judge you for what you did. I promise I don't." He continued to hold her hand as he rounded the desk and came closer to her. He sat on her desk and caressed the back of her hand, starring down at her. "Believe it or not, I get why Marie felt she had to give me up. Women are expected to deal with a lot, not matter what was thrown at them. I get how taking care of the product of her rape was overwhelming for her."

"You do?"

"Yup, and to know that you had been beaten and probably feared for your child's safety forced you to give your son up. Am I right?"

She nodded her head and soon he tilted her chin up to look at him so that he could wipe her face free of the tears and stare into her eyes. "You have to forgive yourself. You did what you thought was best at the time, and am I right to assume that no harm has come to him over the years?"

She nodded her head.

"Good and thank God." He hesitated before he spoke again. "So what will you do now?"

"I'm not sure." She stood up from her seat and stepped back from him. His closeness to her was beginning to send her in overdrive again. "Although I had an idea of it before, hearing you talk about how much you longed to know your birth family growing up has made me wonder if that's how he feels, if he even knows that I exist. I want him to know that I love him, I just felt like I had no other choice than to give him away. And what will you do?"

Andrew laughed. "I know I'm a new creature in Christ and the old me should be dead and gone, but this thing is gonna take more time than what you or anyone else may think it should." Renee gave him a wary look that forged him to continue speaking trying to prove his point to her. "I've already confronted my dad about two times, but I still feel like I just need to break ties with him and the rest of my family if need be."

"For real? You would do that?" Renee frowned.

Andrew rubbed his face. "If I have to. I don't know how much time I need, but as of right now, he can't be in my life. But I know one thing we can and should do."

"What?" Renee raised one eyebrow.

"Don't worry, I wasn't talking about kissing you...just yet. I mean, we can pray. I've missed praying with you."

Renee smiled. "Me, too." She walked and stood in front of him and gathered his hands in hers. "Bow your head."

"No. I'll lead prayer this time." Andrew looked into her eyes.

Renee smiled. "Okay." She bowed her head and squeezed his hands.

"Father God..."

25

Andrew left Renee's office smiling. But more important than the smile on his face, he had peace in his heart that he hadn't since they were last on good terms. He laughed to himself as he opened his car door thinking on how she practically had to put him out of her office. He had more than overstayed his welcome, but he was glad he did. He honestly hadn't meant to let on how much he liked her and that he'd wanted to kiss her for a long time but he couldn't contain his words at the time and he was glad that he didn't.

It felt better to him getting it out in the open. She didn't necessarily respond to him the way he wanted her to but he knew she was shy and given her past relationship with the abusive man, it made sense to him all the more why she felt the need to be guarded.

Since being a part of the men's ministry, he had been continuing to build a relationship with God and his prayer life. He knew he could reach Him on his own, but it was something about his prayers with Renee that just felt right to him, like home, like he belonged with her.

He started up his car and was heading back to his condo, when words from Renee's prayer that she slipped in with his stirred within him. "Lord give us a heart to forgive others and to forgive us of ourselves. Show us the error of our ways so that we may come before you guiltless. We know we're not perfect, but because You've called us to be Holy and imputed righteousness into us, help us to love those who have hurt us and to bless those who have cursed us. Many things don't and haven't made sense to us, but Lord let us not be affected by those things where they stunt our growth in You and our ability to be open and connect with those You've placed in our lives. Help us to be a testimony to others, that no matter what we face, we are able to overcome it because of the love You've shown us and placed inside of us. We are able to live life abundantly despite what we face..." Her prayer moved him as she said it, but it wasn't until his hands guided his steering wheel onto the expressway that led to his parents' home that he fully understood what her prayer had moved him to do.

He prayed to himself in the car right until he parked it in his childhood home's driveway. "Help me, God," he mumbled to himself as he closed the door behind him.

He didn't call ahead to see if they actually were at home, but since Elizabeth had been a stay at home wife and mom all of his life and his dad had recently retired, he reasoned they should be at home. They weren't set to start traveling as they had planned until the summer time. "Are they even still together?" He laughed awkwardly to himself as he stood outside of the door deciding whether or not he should ring the bell or use his key.

He decided on the former, but before he even laid his hand on the button, the door opened and Charles stood on the other side of it.

"Hello, Andrew."

Charles' greeting took a backseat to Andrew's inner thoughts. *Maybe the Lord hasn't worked on me as much as I thought He would have by the time I got here.* Andrew's nostrils flared and he clinched his fists. *I must not be praying hard enough because I still wanna knock this man out.*

His mother appeared as he was trying to calm himself down.

"Hi, Mom." He spoke to her as she brushed past her husband to hug Andrew.

He barely returned her hug as she continued to squeeze him. He could hear soft whimpers as she tried to speak. "I'm so sorry, baby, but I'm so glad you didn't stay away long this time. I love you so much."

"I love you, too." He fully embraced her, squeezing her tightly.

Her whimpering turned into sobbing. "I'm sorry. I'm sorry."

"It's okay, Mom. You didn't do anything wrong." Andrew pulled back from her far enough to look in her face and wipe away some of her tears.

"I'm so glad you came over today." She reached in and squeezed him again.

He smiled. "It's okay, Mom." His nose could sense that she was baking, as well as the apron she wore, so he ushered her back into the kitchen. He finally heard the front door close by the time he crossed the kitchen's threshold.

Elizabeth went and pulled her pan of cookies out of the oven to see how brown they had become. Not satisfied with their color, she put them back in the oven but still leaned over to see if her cake was finally rising. She may not have been crafty but she sure could cook and bake. Hence why Andrew's stomach began to growl. He loved her cakes and cookies and the sweet aroma of vanilla and chocolate in the air reminded him of just how long it had been since he had any of her cooking. At least a year.

Andrew sat at the kitchen table staring around the space. He had so many fond memories of dinners there. Goofing off with Kyle at the table when they should've been focusing on their homework. The room felt much smaller to him than it had when he was growing up, in fact, the entire house did. It didn't hold that same nostalgia it once had for him. That awareness let him know what he needed to finally say to his mom, although he wasn't sure what he'd say to her when he drove to the house and not even when he stood on the doorstep.

"Andrew, talk to me, honey." She noted the pensive look on his face as she wiped her hands on a dish towel before joining him at the table.

He could sense they weren't the only ones in the room and his father's presence was confirmed when he looked over his shoulder to see him leaning against the frame of the entryway of the kitchen.

He knew Charles wanted to speak, as he had always been a very vocal man, but he said nothing.

He gave his dad a smug look before turning back to his mother. "I just came over to do things a little differently than I did the last time."

His father smiled as he approached the table to sit opposite of his son. "So you ready to talk about everything now."

"No. There's nothing more for me to talk to you about." Andrew spoke to him but never looked in Charles' direction.

Elizabeth frowned. "I wish you two could work things out or at least start to."

Andrew's eyes widened as he stared at his mother. "So you two are on good terms? The way you brushed past him at the door, I would've sworn he was your arch enemy. Matter of fact, I wasn't even sure you'd be living here when I stopped by today."

"Well, a phone call could've answered that question." She shifted in her seat and swatted his hand before she became more solemn. "Was I shocked? Hurt? Felt betrayed at the knowledge of what your father did to your birth mother? Yes. Will it take time for me to get past it? Yes. But he's my husband and as crazy as it may sound to you, I still love him."

Andrew scooted back from the table after her last words registered in his head.

She reached for him, forcing him to place his hand in hers.

"Andrew, I never met the man that raped Marie. I've only known the strict yet loving, kind-hearted, and generous man that is your father. That's the man that I know. He's told me everything now and we're working to get past it. While I don't like his past and I hate what he did to Marie," her voice quivered, "he's still my husband, your father."

Choosing his words carefully, Andrew stared at her as he spoke, "I'm not sure what I expected you to say or do after you found out, but I know what I have to do. I can't be around you all anymore."

"Andrew, no." She covered her mouth with one hand and squeezed his hand as tight as she could with her other hand.

"Ma, if you're gonna stay here with him, then I can't be around you anymore." He stood up but she continued squeezing his hand. He reached down and planted a tender, lingering kiss on her cheek. "I really do love you, Ma. You're in covenant with him, but I'm not. I can't continue to be the best man I can be and mature into an even better one if he's in my life. I can only grow with people who have integrity." He finally pulled his hand from her grasp as she lowered her head and whimpered.

Charles stood up from the table. "Son, let me make things right with you." There was a deep seated sense of desperation in his voice.

Andrew finally made eye contact with his dad. "Charles, you knew how long I wanted to know my birth mother and father. I never discredited you all, but remember all of the nights we sat up in the den talking about life? My biggest dream of uniting both of my families together. All along you knew a truth about it I didn't and yet you never told me. Not that I would've loved Charles Jr. and Lisa any more than I could have growing up had I known they were my blood siblings, but to hide that from me, too? I have no respect for you. Makes no sense for me to be around you with how little I care for you." He turned his attention away from Charles and back to Elizabeth. "Ma, maybe in a few months I'll be in a different head space and you can come visit me at my house, but right now I just need to distance myself from y'all. Bye." He turned and lowered his head as he walked out of the kitchen and out of the house.

Elizabeth wept loudly as Charles slammed the table with both hands before dropping his head. His tears hit the light wood grained table.

26

"Why are you staring at me like that?" Renee struggled to keep eye contact with Andrew under his intense stare. At work, she was just a social worker reading through files and making house visits when need be, but with Andrew, he reminded her that she was a woman. He awakened a part of her that she hadn't experienced since she had first met Ted and didn't know what kind of man he really was.

Andrew smirked and stared at her fidgeting with the napkin on the table, her hair, and just about anything else she could to help keep her attention off him. He finally spoke up, sensing she was still waiting for the answer to her question. "Why shouldn't I look at you? You're beautiful."

She smiled but turned her head. *What do I have to be embarrassed about?* She answered her own question by sitting straight up in her seat and fixing a comfortable stare on him.

He laughed. "Okay, I see. Either you're daring me to stop looking at you or you finally decided to accept my compliment."

She could no longer keep a straight face with him and the corners of her mouth curved up before she finally let out a soft laugh.

"Yes!" He pumped his fist in the air. "I made you smile and laugh."

She shook her head but continued smiling at him.

"Okay, I just find it interesting that although we've known each other for a minute and talk again all of the time, this is our first time together out somewhere other than the cafe."

She looked around at the dimly lit restaurant, heard the clanking of glassware, rather than the sound of an espresso machine revving up to produce a caffeinated delight for a waiting customer. She looked down at her clothes and saw that it was the most modern and sexy outfit she had worn to date with him. The form fitting, multicolored, knee-length dress hugged curves of hers she didn't even know she had. It laid well over her coca cola bottle shaped frame.

"Yes."

He pulled her attention away from herself.

"And yes, you're not wearing a jean skirt with a not so flattering top." He feigned coughing as he said the last of his statement. He grabbed his glass of water and sipped some to complete his choking act.

"Oh whatever. You're not choking, I heard you. I decided to ditch the skirt and not so flattering top, as you said, for this." With her hands, she spanned the part of her body he could see. She laughed.

"What?"

"Well, it's more like Kim made me ditch my regular clothing when she found out you were actually gonna pick me up from my house." Renee switched her voice to sound more like Kim's stark voice. "She said, 'Mrs. Doubtfire, he asked you out on a date, so you have to look the part.' I told her it wasn't a date. She is a trip." Renee was still giggling and continued on not noting that Andrew was no longer laughing with her. "After rummaging through my closet and not finding anything to her liking, she came out of her purse with this number." She finally looked up to see the serious look on his face. "What's wrong?"

"You."

"Hunh?" She raised an eyebrow.

"Why can't this be a date?"

"I don't know, maybe because you didn't say it was a date when you invited me out tonight. I don't want to assume anything." She bit her lip and began to fidget with her napkin on the table again.

"So I tell you to wear something more formal than normal, I show up at your place in a suit and with flowers, and escort you here to this, might I add, romantic restaurant. I mean look, linen napkins." He picked up and dropped his napkin on the table. "Soft lights. A pianist playing Babyface and Brian McKnight songs. Come on now, those two?" He cocked his head at her.

Renee giggled at his hand gestures and 'are you kidding me' facial expressions.

"We're not at the cafe eating salads and Paninis and sipping on lattes. How could this not be a date?"

Renee looked around the room taking in everything and what he had said. She looked back to him. "Because when you called, you didn't say," she pretended to hold a phone up to her ear, "'Hey, Renee, can I take you on a date Thursday night when I get back from my trip?' Nope, you didn't say that to me." Renee stared at him matter-of-factly.

Their eyes lingered with one another before Andrew finally decided to address what she said. "You know what? You're right. I feel like this is our first date, but at the same time I'm scared to call it that because we both still have some major issues we're working through. I don't want us to skip continuing to build a solid foundation as friends and rush into a relationship only to have my 'daddy' issues and your 'baby daddy and kid' issues hinder us from really growing together romantically. Do you get what I'm saying?" He stared at her.

She reluctantly nodded her head.

"I can't afford to not have you in my life because I screw up something romantic with you and you cast me off like that guy that did you wrong." He looked at her saddened countenance. "I'm sorry for bringing him up."

"No, you weren't. He was a dirt bag." They both laughed before locking eyes with one another again. She broke her trance from him to finish her statement, "I'm honestly over him, but you're right about my 'kid' issues." She held up air quotes. "I really do wanna be a part of his life."

He saw her retreating into herself. Instead of letting her slip away from him, he pulled on her hand she was slowly sliding off of the table. He gripped it and began to caress the back of it as his eyes pleaded with hers to look into his. When they finally settled into a comfortable stare, he continued speaking, "Please don't shut me out. What are you gonna do about the kid?"

She perked up some with a glimmer of hope. "Well technically, even though I know a lot about him because of all the info Marcus found out for me, I couldn't dare use any of it in a legal case to win him back or at least rights to see him. I've talked to some people above me to see what I can do and I've been doing some research of my own. While I don't know if it'll fly, I'm hoping I can file for having given him up under duress and go from there."

"Technically you were. And if there's anything you need me to do or help you with, you can count on me. Although my connects are mainly business and entertainment people, I do have an old college buddy who I know studied family law and the last time I linked up with him, I found out that he was a shark in the field. His win rate is well above ninety-five percent."

She paused looking at him. An internal conversation began brewing in her. *I devoted my life even more so to God and prayer after Ted and giving up my son as a way of recompense, but I think this man is trying to make me see that I can still live for God and have the right man in my life. But we aren't ready for each other yet. Are we?* She dismissed her inner thoughts as Andrew's high arching eyebrows prompted her to speak aloud to him again. "Thanks. Even though I'm checking to see if I can possibly get him back, I'm still not sure if I should." She breathed a deep sigh but shifted her thoughts to him. "And what about you? I know when we were on the phone while you were gone the past week you mentioned that you had told your parents you were cutting them out of your life. You think that's reasonable? Do you think God is pleased with your decision?"

He smiled at her. "See, I'm getting better. Weeks ago, if someone would've brought my dad up, I would've snapped, but I'm calmer now." He took a deep breath and slowly exhaled. "Is my staying away from him and my mom the best and most mature thing? Maybe not, to some people. But, it makes sense to me for now. Am I supposed to forgive him and not hold a grudge against him? Of course, I'm supposed to let go and let God. Forgive my dad because God had forgiven me of so much? I'm certain I'm supposed to, but I'm not there yet. And rather than thinking such evil thoughts whenever I'm around him and actually putting my hands on him, I'd rather just keep my distance from him until, when, and if I allow God to soften my heart towards him."

"Andrew, God answers prayers and prayer can change anything. It's up to the believer to continue to believe God to answer the prayer." She took a deep breath wondering why she hadn't yet heeded her own words. "The road to getting our prayers answered may require certain actions to be followed. Not heeding God's advice may delay the manifestation of the answer to the prayer."

He buried the weight of Renee's words in the recesses of his mind, but was prompted to speak to the beauty in front of him. "So you'll be taking your own advice, right?" he said with a sly smile on his face.

Her spirit lifted again and she laughed looking at him. "Whatever, but you're right, we can't be together until you resolve your 'daddy' issues." She playfully snarled at him.

His gaping mouth and wide eyes let her know that he was shocked by her statement.

"You know I'm telling the truth. You already said the same."

"I guess I can't argue with that, but this is going to be hard."

"What?" She nodded her head letting the waiter know that he could take her plate away. She hadn't eaten much from it anyway. Andrew dared her to live a little and try the lobster. It didn't taste bad to her, it was her first time trying it and she had just been so nervous with him for the earlier part of their dinner and then so intrigued with their conversation that it had gotten cold. She had told herself that certainly cold lobster was nasty, but Andrew must have thought otherwise.

"Would you please prepare hers to go?" he said as the waiter grabbed his empty plate also. "What?" He looked at Renee. "You may want to eat it later, if not, coming to pick it up from you will give me another reason to come see you."

"You need another reason?" She playfully pouted with a glint of humor in her eyes.

"See, this is gonna be hard."

"What?"

"Us just being friends."

Her forehead creased with confusion. "Why do you think that?"

"Because, you already know I think you're beautiful."

She temporarily averted eye contact with him before reminding herself it was safe to look into his eyes.

"Thank you." He appreciated her finding comfort with him. "You are very compassionate, intelligent, God-fearing, humble, I could go on and on. You have so many qualities that make me like you, care for you so much." He let his words rest in the air hoping that she would know he was nothing like her ex, never planned to be. When he saw her smile brighten, he continued, "I definitely wanna be more than just friends with you, but we both agreed that we have some unfinished business to attend to before we can make us tight and right." He continued caressing the back of her hand that he had never let go from earlier. He reached across the table and with his eyes implored that she put her other hand in his. When she finally did, her wrists loosened. She heaved a sigh he thought was relief and he felt her completely relax in his presence. "Okay, tomorrow is Friday, the close of the business week. Think we can get our issues solved by the close of the business day so we can start dating this weekend?" He smiled before they both exploded in laughter and ignoring the inquisitive stares of patrons nearby.

Other Books Available

Sisterhood Chronicles Series
Underneath It All
Discovery
Untold
When It Happens To You
All Things Considered

Forever Friends Series
Catch Me If You Can
It's Complicated

Limelight Series
Hues
Tones
Vision

Standalone Titles
After All Is Said & Done
The Bid Catcher: Distinguished Gentlemen Series

(Best if you read Forever Friends series before reading Sisterhood Chronicles 3)

COMING SOON

The Kissing Game: Love Alive 1

ABOUT THE AUTHOR

Anita Davis is a former elementary teacher born and raised in Chicago. Although she wrote short stories much of her childhood, she didn't unlock and cultivate her passion as a writer until she became a writing teacher for middle school students. The more she had to create sample writings for her students, the more she realized her passion and ability to tell stories in the written form. She decided to hone her craft as a writer by completing her Master of Fine Arts in Creative Writing via National University. She now pursues writing books most of her time, in addition to being a flight attendant. Anita seeks to encourage, engage, and entertain her readers.

She is Co-Founder of Book Euphoria, a group of Chicago authors bound by their love of literature. Book Euphoria hosts literary events and they also founded the empowerment movement, Black Girl Passion.

Anita writes contemporary romantic women's fiction and seeks to encourage, engage, and entertain her readers.

authoranitadavis@gmail.com
www.authoranitadavis.com
Facebook: Anita Davis and Author page: Author Anita Davis
Instagram: @authoranitadavis   Twitter: @_AnitaDavis

www.ingramcontent.com/pod-product-compliance
Lightning Source LLC
Chambersburg PA
CBHW060515180626
46817CB00002B/367